-30-

A novella by
Clinton W. Waters

Copyright © 2020 Clinton W. Waters

All rights reserved.

ISBN-13: 9798568454984

....

*TO ALEX, WHOSE DREAM PLANTED THE SEED
FOR THIS STORY*

....

CONTENTS

1 Morning   1

2 Day   19

3 Night   63

....

Morning

The door creaked open and so did Greg's eyelids. It was blue dawn and socked feet padded their way past his back to the foot of the bed. Greg's phone illuminated his cocoon of comforter, alerting him that his Ephemera, Joe, had arrived. Joe was putting his jacket on the back of the chair at Greg's desk. "Right on time," Greg groaned. They had agreed on the terms of their engagement a few days prior, and Joe was holding true to them. It had felt odd to Greg, giving a stranger the code to get into his apartment. But then again, this was all a little strange.

"You don't get five stars by being late," Joe whispered. Greg could hear the smile in his voice and it made his stomach sweetly sour. How long had it been since someone new was in his bedroom? Leftover dreams clung to the corners of his mind as he rubbed his eyes. When he opened them again, he saw that Joe's stomach was sky blue in the pale light of the morning, his shirt lifting up and over his head. He folded it and draped it over his jacket. His belt buckle clinked as he undid the clasp, jingling as he took off his pants and folded them neatly. He laid them over the back of the chair as well.

Checking the time, Greg did some foggy-brained math and determined he had only gotten a few hours of sleep. Unable to feel tired for the anxiety of it all, he had performed the cardinal sin of trying to do research online, as if that would put his mind at ease. He had done so well up until that point, only the occasional deep dive every few years. He read articles and seriously considered buying some ebooks on the matter. Bombarded by ads for life insurance with sad songs about heaven, he gave up. He wound up at the same conclusion everyone had told him for years. It would never make sense. There would be no correlation. No demographic data that skewed one way or the other. No probability model of lifestyle or location that could give him an honest answer. It all amounted to 50-50.

A coin that had been spinning mid-air for 30 years.

He chuckled to himself at that thought. He was showing his age. Coins. What a novel concept.

Greg sank a little towards the middle of the mattress as Joe sat on the side. "May I join you?" he asked. He turned to look at Greg over his shoulder, which was mottled with pale freckles, tiny hairs glowing as the blue gave way to red and orange. Greg was surprised at how broad Joe was, taller and larger than he had imagined from his pictures on the Ephemera app. He had little love handles that rested above the waistband of his boxers, dark pink stretch marks rising up from below. Greg lifted the comforter and Joe slid in so that they were face to face. The comforter descended again and plunged them into darkness. Just Greg's morning breath mingling with the coffee clinging to Joe's teeth..

"Happy Birthday," Joe said quietly.

"What's so happy about it?" Greg asked, his voice gravelly. He had paid for an entire day. The moment he woke up until just past midnight that night. Had paid extra to ensure midnight was included in their allotted time. From there, whether Greg disappeared or went on living didn't matter. They'd never see each other again. Maybe it never mattered, he thought to himself.

"It's yours, for one," Joe said. He placed a leg over Greg's and pulled up the hem of Greg's shirt, resting his hand on Greg's side. Greg jerked at the cold of it and they both laughed. He felt a bit of the awkwardness ebb away. But this stranger, this Joe was in a spot that had belonged to someone else.

"What about for two?" Greg asked.

"For two, you have me," Joe said into the darkness. Greg's phone illuminated again, a happy birthday text from Avni. Of course she'd be texting him this early. He felt a little silly, but the thought did occur to him that he was excited for her to meet Joe. Maybe that equated to showing Joe off, which didn't make him feel great. But then again, wasn't that a perk of having him in the first place?

Bathed in the dull white glow, Greg begrudgingly admitted to himself how handsome Joe was. How that had been a major factor in choosing which Ephemera he'd spend his 30th birthday with. But more than how attractive he was, Greg felt he "looked" like a boyfriend. The kind who had family out west and had bad taste in music, but called it artistic. Someone to crawl into bed in the wee hours of the morning and stick his cold mitts on your stomach. The kind of guy Greg would take to dinner at his mom's house (an event he would absolutely dread, but Joe would genuinely look forward to). For a moment, the cell phone's light reflected in Joe's dark eyes, and he thought of looking across the table at him and giving him a pained look as his mother veered into politics. He was taking a memory of Zeke and imposing Joe on top of it. It was working perhaps too well.

The light grew dim and shut off, waking Greg up from his daydream.

He thought of the reality. Saying goodbye to his mother the day before. Just in case. Asking her not to come to the party. The pain in her eyes, how her lips grew thin with the effort of biting her tongue. Him bringing up the only other party they had both been at, Alissa's, four years ago.

He took a deep breath and sighed at this.

"And for three, I have the whole day planned out," Joe said, "nothing for you to worry about." This was part of their ruse, however. A line he had given Joe to feed him. Greg had actually planned the entire day, more or less. But Joe was going to handle everything. Carry the bags. Help him decorate for the party. Greg began to think about the party then, his heart beating a little quicker. God, there was so much left to do. "Hey," Joe said, almost sternly. "Don't spend today worrying, okay?" he said, his hand roving under Greg's shirt. He drew Greg closer to him, his lips finding Greg's in the dark. He kissed him softly, their lips just barely brushing. Greg returned the gesture with force, bringing a hand up to rest on the back of Joe's head. Greg felt as though he should pull away. This was all a lie. A lie he had paid for. But he was ashamed at how quickly his body was ready to accept it, felt starved and wretched. His face grew hot, embarrassed at how pitiful he was. Paying for someone else's company. Joe squeezed him and he said, "Okay?" in a deep grumble.

"Okay," Greg said, relenting and burying his face in Joe's neck. He had the sudden urge to cry. Why not, he figured. He may not have that many opportunities left.

"It will be a good day," Joe said. His arms softened from grip to comforting embrace. "I promise," he whispered. What a way to ruin the mood, Greg thought to himself as he blubbered. But maybe he was a little grateful, a little glad sex wasn't the first thing they did together.

The sun had officially climbed over the horizon by the time Greg's tears ran dry. Joe kissed him on the forehead and slid out of bed. Greg finally emerged from the comforter, eyes red and puffy. "I'm going to get started on breakfast," Joe said, reaching for his clothes.

"Don't," Greg said. Joe smiled and bowed his head slightly. He stood and left. A few moments later Greg heard the clattering of dishes. Greg pulled himself out of bed and stood at his window for a moment. The world outside was well awake by now. Fat flakes of snow were falling lazily from the sky and Greg felt a surge of happiness. He had really been hoping to see snow on his birthday. He found his e-cig and took a deep puff, blowing a strawberry-scented haze over the glass.

The cars on the street hummed along like a school of fish,

sliding in and out of intersections seamlessly. He spied on people's windshields sometimes, catching whatever lowered opacity show or report was playing out while they put on their makeup, texted their friends. He yawned and stretched. How grateful he was to not be getting ready for work. Running to catch the subway, sweating through his business casual attire. All the rush just to hurdle headlong towards another eight hour day of recording sales figures for whatever it was they were hocking that month.

His "Good Luck" party had been a joke, as they usually are. He had always been a little weirded out by them in the first place, having endured a few in his time with the company. He understood they couldn't have a traditional going away party, in case the person in question might show back up on Monday. But they also couldn't just ask them to pack their things and fire them for having a birthday. They did effectively do that to everyone, including him, of course. The head of HR herself met him at his cubicle as he came in for the day, a fairly small box at her side. "The big 3-0," she said nervously and handed him the box. He was slow on the uptake, so she added, so very helpfully, "For all your things," gesturing at his desk. Greg looked from her to his desk, where his work display lay blank, wiped clean. It appeared they had scrubbed all the surfaces as well, going around his "things". No trace of him would remain. They were sure of that.

Greg packed away the few personalizing touches he had kept in his cubicle. A picture frame that rotated through some old pictures: him and Zeke, him with his mother and Alissa, him and Avni, clearly drunk. The card Peter had gotten him for his birthday the year before joined the frame in the box. Lastly, a Maneki-neko statue Zeke had brought him back from Japan, but Greg couldn't really stand to have at home. It waved at him cheerfully. The box suddenly seemed huge with only three things in it. He could have just brought a grocery tote, really. The HR Manager tapped her toes and checked her watch. She tsked at an email or text that came across its screen. "Finished?" she asked, and he really thought she was being earnest. Greg looked down at the empty desk and the mostly empty box and stammered that he was. She said, "Very good."

Once his little corner of the world was packed away, she escorted him to that floor's break room. More or less a closet with a water dispenser and a coffee maker. A fridge people liked to steal his lunches out of. His department members were crammed in, standing around the tiny table, which had a cake at its center. It was apparent it was a template cake from the grocery, meant for a baby shower or birthday. "Good Luck, Craig" was scrawled on it in red icing. No one addressed this. A piece was already missing from the edge. No one addressed this either. They raised their respective mugs or water bottles in a kind of salute to him.

Most of them would be happy to see him gone, he thought. He felt he was good at his job, but the last year had been rough. Most people didn't have a lot of patience for him, or anyone, to begin with. But he threw a wrench in some pivotal deals by missing work. He assumed they were all thinking of this as they sat staring at him, slowly bringing their mugs to their lips. Greg began to feel like he had showed up to a wolf den, leering eyes and lips curling to reveal sickle fangs. Waiting for him to wobble. One misstep and they'd go for the throat. Mercifully, Peter poked his head in the doorway, a little breathless. A sight for sore eyes.

"Did I miss anything?" Peter asked him.

"Nope!" Greg said, trying to plead to him with his eyes to just end this hellscape.

"Good, good," Peter said. He explained he got caught up in a client meeting and time got away from him. He was like a dandelion pushing out of a crack in the sidewalk. Suddenly, people loosened up a little bit. Arguably, that was as loose as they could get. Some smiles. Peter made sure to point out the time Greg worked so late he bumped into the custodial robot. Greg remembered that. It had scared the shit out of him, purring as it rolled out of a shadow in the corner. It tripped an alarm in the robot, which sent the footage to Peter and the other managers for the floor. With Greg's permission, he shared it with the others. Greg knew this was also a subtle dig at the others, proving to them how dedicated Greg had been. Peter had pushed for Greg to get promotions. It wasn't his fault they never happened. In general, Peter was passionate about under 30's getting treated like people, but it wasn't a common sentiment in their field. From what he gathered from his friends, it wasn't a popular opinion in any field. They were young, the management believed, being hungry would make them work harder. To Greg's mind, the entire building could burn down and the only thing worth saving would be Peter.

People eventually started to trickle away. Productivity couldn't be reduced too much, Greg knew. People had birthdays every year. It didn't call for an extra long break. For once, Greg was grateful for the corporate clock watching. At one point, Peter leaned in and asked quietly, "Who the hell is Craig?". Greg gave him a defeated sigh and they shared a subdued laugh together.

After about an hour of stale coffee and even more stale small talk, enough people had returned to work that Greg felt he could leave. The HR Manager returned the lid to cover what was left of the cake and put it into Greg's box. He tried to refuse but she insisted, walking out of the break room and looking back at him expectantly. He had to be escorted to the door. Peter walked alongside Greg, the HR Manager on his other side. Peter told him some details about a client they worked on together, for when he came back. He said he really appreciated all the hard work, but Greg should enjoy the time off. Greg knew Peter was speaking from the heart, but was also trying hard not to acknowledge the blade that loomed over Greg's head. No hysterical crying or anything, but he got a solid hug. Some well wishes that held more sincerity than those given by the entirety of the office added together. Peter said he'd be at the party, so he would save the sentimental stuff for then. When Peter left, the HR Manager shook his hand and held the door open, gesturing for him to walk ahead. "We hope to see you Monday," she said and immediately stepped back in so the door swung shut. He wasn't certain, but he thought he heard the deadbolt latch. She stood watching him from inside the door until he had driven off.

He hadn't bothered unpacking the box from the office. Except for the tatters of cake, of course, which he had promptly put in the refrigerator and forgotten about. He stared at the box now, jammed into the corner of his room. It practically oozed out a gray aura of "let's circle back to that," paired with a miasma of "I'm just confused as to why...."

His phone dinged and he grabbed it off the bed, expecting another text. It was an email this time, from the city. Its subject line read, "Happy Birthday! Some Things to Remember!" The header featured the police's mascot, a happy looking cartoon dog named Spot. Mouth wide, tongue out. Spot was fond of saying things like, "If you spot some trouble, call the authorities!" Greg watched the cartoon as a kid, where Spot would track down bad guys and after a dust cloud fight scene they'd be handcuffed and on their way to jail.

The Spot from the email had a little speech bubble that read, "Happy Birthday!" Below that there was an image of Spot, more serious now, his happy-go-lucky tongue no longer lolling out of his mouth. He said, "But remember to be responsible." That was followed by a brief bulleted list of things Greg should avoid doing for the remainder of the day, but especially towards midnight. Operating non-AI machinery, including bicycles. Performing any crime with the thinking you won't be around to face the consequences. Do anything abnormally or uncharacteristically dangerous.

Failure to adhere to these guidelines could result in a fine that must be paid by your closest living relative. He thought of his mother again, clutching her phone to her chest when she received the email.

She would likely find it sentimental somehow. Greg's last gift to her. A message from beyond. Wherever he might end up. At the end of the email, Spot was surrounded by floating hearts that had been animated to drift up and away. "Remember," he said, "you are loved!" Finally, the email ended with a hotline number to call if you were feeling...uncharacteristically dangerous. He understood the appeal of certain things at this point. If he were to ever rob a bank, today would be the day. But no, he thought, he'd rather wait and take his chances with whatever fate grew closer with every minute.

Greg took a sobering breath and smelled the coffee Joe had put on. He meandered into the kitchen, somewhat bashful. "Sorry about that," Greg said as Joe dropped a piece of french toast into the skillet and the sizzle filled the air. Joe turned, wearing only Greg's apron over his underwear. Greg couldn't help but feel bolstered by this.

"Don't be," Joe said, smiling. Greg wondered if the smile was as genuine as it seemed or if he was just being good at his job. He thought about this as he retrieved his many medications from their little cabinet cave above the oven. Purple to quell anxiety, red to stabilize his mood, pink to keep the dark thoughts away. He tossed the confetti of solid chemicals into the back of his mouth and swallowed them down. Any of them could easily have the opposite effect than what was intended. But the prospect of not taking them was just as bad. Held hostage by his own brain, was the way he often thought of it. And held hostage by the city-assigned therapist he saw once a month. Monitoring his progress, they said.

"I saw a cake in your fridge," Joe said. "Who is Craig?" Greg laughed and tried to explain the work party. But the longer he talked, he realized Joe wasn't turning to look at him or really engaging in the conversation. Greg said maybe it was just one of those "you had to be there" moments.

Joe didn't say anything, busy with his own work. Greg felt he was intentionally not watching, a flinching away from something ugly. It told himself he was being paranoid. But he felt a ghost standing just behind Joe, its head shaking slightly in shame. It was reality, reminding him that anything Greg did was an occupational hazard for Joe. Something he dealt with to get his paycheck.

He decided he couldn't leave it alone.

"Do your clients often cry?" Greg asked, leaning on the counter. He noticed Joe had tucked a small suitcase beneath the bar. He probably wouldn't have noticed it if he wasn't keeping his eyes trained on the ground. Joe was committed to sliding into the stream of Greg's life uninterrupted, it seemed, another fish joining the school.

"I don't think you want to talk about my other clients," Joe said, flipping the toast. His voice had the strained quality of a sober friend helping a drunk one. You don't really want to text your ex. If you think about it, you won't feel good after eating $20 worth of fast food.

"What if I do?" Greg asked, straightening up.

"You don't," Joe said quietly, turning to look him in the eye. They stared at one another for a moment, Joe's face impassive. The bubbling and popping french toast batter provided the only sound to disrupt the silence. A streak of heat ran up Greg's neck. "T.V., play

'Drummond House'," Joe said. "They released the finale last night. Figured we could watch it over breakfast."

"That's fortunate timing," Greg said, trying to recover his resolve. "And nice of you to remember."

"That's what I'm here for." Joe's smile returned. Greg knew this knowledge had come from a questionnaire he filled out when he signed up for Ephemera and listed the job. Joe had a small retinue of seemingly useless facts to help sell him as a committed lover or an erstwhile friend. He supposed he should feel flattered or relieved somehow that Joe had taken the time to actually read the thing, had committed at least some of it to memory. "Go relax, I'll bring it to you," Joe said, and Greg realized he had been staring at Joe the whole time.

The intro to Drummond House poured softly out of the television in the living room. Greg sunk into the couch, pulling his legs up to sit cross-legged. "I'll admit I've never watched any of it," Joe said, bringing him a plate of french toast laden with syrup and powdered sugar. He placed a cup of coffee, pale brown with cream and sugar, on the coffee table. He took the apron off and brought his own plate, sitting directly beside Greg, knees wide, resting against him. Greg noted how the bottom hem of Joe's boxers slightly creased against his thigh.

"It's just trashy reality stuff," Greg said, peeling his eyes off of Joe's leg. He took a bite of the french toast and commented on how delicious it was.

"I'm not too shabby in the kitchen," Joe said, picking up an entire piece of the toast and stuffing the sugary mess into his mouth. "Tell me about the show," he said past his food, "I want to know."

"It's one of those where they compete for a bunch of money. But the challenge is just to live like people used to. No electricity, no running water." He took a sip of his coffee. "They basically live in a castle and bitch about not having toilet paper," he said. Joe laughed at this, watching the T.V. intently. Greg felt a little flutter in his stomach. He could make Joe laugh. It felt like a gold star, and he felt equally childish.

Nevertheless, Greg watched Joe watching the show and a smile crept up on him. They ate together in a cozy pastiche, "Lovers Reclining at Breakfast" or something to that effect. In that moment he wished, as he often found himself wishing at certain parts of his life, that he could get a freeze frame of this moment. This calm, quiet moment he couldn't resist shattering like the stillness of a lake's surface. The show went to commercial and Greg cleared his throat. "So, Joe," Greg began and Joe grunted in ascent, tucking away another piece of the toast. "What if I seriously wanted to talk to you about your job. Isn't that how I get to know you?"

"What job do you want me to have? I have a few I've practiced making small talk about. Being an accountant is an old fall back. Or maybe you want me to be your personal trainer?" Joe ran a hand up Greg's thigh.

"No, I mean your job as an Ephemera," Greg said. Joe withdrew his hand and went back to eating. "I want to know you, not come up with someone for you to be."

Joe took his time chewing and washed it down with some coffee. He set his plate on the coffee table and said, "T.V., pause." The T.V. beeped in compliance and the contestants stopped their bickering. Joe turned so that his whole body was facing Greg. "This isn't about getting to know me. This is about you and your day," he said and placed a hand on Greg's knee, gripping it slightly. "I am here to make you happy and that's what I intend to do. This isn't always a happy job and talking about it won't make you happy." He gave Greg a weak smile, practically begging him to drop it.

"Is it that it will make me unhappy or it will make you unhappy?" Greg asked, setting his plate on the table as well. "I feel that as your client I should know about your past experience." He was the paying customer here, if he wanted to talk about it they would. A piece of him knew that's what the review system on the Ephemera app was for. Obviously it had meant something to him, as he vividly recalled a review that called Joe the perfect companion.

"We both know what this is," Joe said. "Acknowledging it will only serve to ruin the illusion." He stood and collected their plates. "It's not love, but it doesn't have to feel transactional." He began to turn away but stopped. "Also," he said, talking down into the plates, "just because you have paid for my time doesn't mean you own me."

"I never said that," Greg said, his face going flush.

"If you want to know about my other clients, you're not the first to act this way." Joe leveled an even gaze on him, no malice or ill intent, but stern all the same. "Whatever you've been through or might go through dealing with your birthday, it's a lot. But it's coming either way."

"What if getting to know you will help distract me? Enhance my experience?" Greg asked, standing.

Joe made it to the kitchen and raked the plates clear. He sighed deeply, gripping the sink and leaning over it. "How about this. You can ask me questions and I will choose whether or not I want to respond. Deal?"

"Deal," Greg said, coming up beside him.

"But no more for now," Joe said, standing to his full height, practically looming over Greg. Greg nodded. "I have a surprise for you." Joe went to the suitcase and opened one of the exterior pockets. "I wanted it to be your good luck charm from me, but I think it might be better served right now." He made Greg close his eyes and hold out his hands. A slick rectangular box with sharp edges fell into his palm. He cautiously opened his eyes to see a pack of cigarettes.

"Did you really?" Greg asked, greedily ripping off the cellophane. "Where did you find them?" He opened the top of the pack and inhaled deeply. The menthol was old but pungent, slightly burning the inside of his nose.

"I have my connections," Joe said slyly. He reached into the pack and pulled one out, flipping it around and sticking it back in. "There. A lucky one for you. People used to do that, right?" Greg pulled another out and began looking around for something to light it. He hadn't had need for a lighter in years. "Are you going to smoke it in here?" Joe asked incredulously. He dug a box of matches out of the suitcase as well and lit it, cupping the flame and lighting Greg's cigarette.

"Why not?" Greg said, holding the cigarette in the corner of his mouth. He did his best to look at Joe with a Dietrich or Bogart half-lid. Too cool to care. "I might not get the security deposit back anyway." He took a small draw, his body instantly awash in the nicotine. It was incredibly stale, but it had probably been packaged a decade ago. He was still grateful and decided to keep his mouth shut and just enjoy it. This was a gesture he hadn't scripted, a present he couldn't have seen coming. "It's a problem for tomorrow me," he said, trying his best to strike a pose with the cigarette. If there's a tomorrow me, he thought.

"That's the spirit," Joe said, smiling. Greg offered it to him and he took a puff. It was obvious he'd never smoked a "real" cigarette, but he assumed not many people had at this point. He handed it back, coughing and laughing.

A loud, jarring chirp sounded from the ceiling and a cordial, if not dry, voice piped into the room. "Attention resident of apartment 452, smoke has been detected. Authorities will be alerted-"

"False alarm!" Greg called out, trying hard not to laugh, waving his hand through the smoke to disperse it. "Burnt breakfast," he said.

The ceiling chimed more agreeably this time. "Please report any damage immediately for maintenance and billing review. Thank you." Greg ashed the cigarette in the sink and smiled at Joe. "What's next on the agenda?" he asked. He hazarded a glance at the oven clock. They were behind schedule. He knew next would be going to get food for the party.

"Figured we'd go to the museum," Joe said, going back into the bedroom. Greg drew the very last bit of smoke from the cigarette and ran some water over it. The cherry let out one final guttural hiss before going out completely.

"The museum?" Greg asked, unsure. He followed Joe and found him pulling his shirt over his head.

"The museum," Joe said matter-of-factly as he slid his pants back on. "They've just opened." He picked a few random things from the closet for Greg to put on. He grabbed a red scarf - Zeke's scarf - from the closet and tossed it to him. "It's chilly out there."

DAY

Joe wasn't wrong. Snow had started to pile up on parked cars and synthetic bushes lining the street. Although the sky was gloomy, it was hard for Greg not to feel slightly warm and fuzzy. His hand firmly grasped in Joe's, they took their time walking past window displays. Faceless families sat frozen on their perpetual Christmas morning. "If you want to go in anywhere, just say the word," Joe leaned over and said to him. The truth was, Greg had spent most of his paltry savings on this day with Joe. Not to mention he'd just be buying things for other people. More stuff to account for when he was gone. If he was gone, he tried to correct himself. But it didn't stick.

They descended to the subway, navigating its labyrinth of turnstiles and escalators. A violinist was busking at their platform, her case propped up on a bench beside her. She wasn't playing anything Christmas related, which Greg was incredibly thankful for. He'd been working on Christmas ads at work since the Fourth of July. He wanted every carol torn up and roasted on an open fire at that point. There was a code sticker on its shell, which Greg scanned with his phone's camera. It took him to a site which had her information and a money app link to leave tips. He sent her a couple of bucks. She bowed slightly, the jet black violin still tucked between her chin and shoulder.

"That was nice of you," Joe said.

"Eh," Greg said and shrugged. "I won't have any use for money after tonight." He watched the train approach the platform. A brief "Call of the Void" moment came to him. He assumed the train would be quick. He could be done with the agony of anticipation. After 30 long years of it, he still wasn't prepared. Joe placed his arm around Greg, which snapped him out of his thoughts.

"You'll regret that come tomorrow when you have to figure out where rent's coming from," Joe said, smirking. "And that smoke damage fee," he said with a wink. The train screeched to a halt and the doors slid open. Not many people coming or going, it seemed. Everyone was trying to stay out of the cold, Greg guessed. Joe walked them past a few cars until he found an empty one, or so he thought. Once the doors closed and the train jerked to life again, Greg noticed a squat little robot, diligently buffering a splash of graffiti. It paused and doused the area with more cleaning solution, then went back to scrubbing. Greg smiled to himself, as the robot itself was peppered with stickers, cartoon dicks, and hastily scrawled permanent marker initials. "A + A Forever", "For a good time call".

Once they were deep in the tunnels, awash in the sickly yellow of the train car lights, Joe moved his hand onto Greg's thigh. "What are you doing?" Greg asked.

"No one's around," Joe said quietly, but it felt like he was yelling. Greg's eyes darted to the sanitation robot. "So?" Joe asked and moved his hand a little higher. Greg remembered this game from school. Are You Nervous. He felt the same shameful pang he felt then. When every touch carried an extra thousand pounds of nuance. Yes, I'm nervous but what if I don't want you to stop? What does that say about me? When does everyone else chicken out? What if I'm dying to know what happens when you go just a little further up?

"Quit," Greg said and brushed Joe's hand away. Joe complied. "Those things do have cameras you know."

"So does most everything," Joe said and shrugged. "Can't deny yourself just 'cause someone may be watching." He looked at the robot and grinned. "Maybe they like to watch."

"Do you write copy for ecards?" Greg asked sarcastically. "Or motivational company emails?"

"Do you want me to?" Joe asked. Greg took this as an attempt to joke about their conversation earlier. He let out a fake laugh, but didn't respond. Instead, he just listened to the rattle of the car. The high-pitched whine of metal wheels against metal tracks. The squeak of the robot's efforts. He was still getting used to this. A microwave meal relationship. None of the set up, none of the mess. Just instant gratification. So why couldn't he just let himself be gratified?

As the train began to slow for their stop, Greg snuck a glance over at Joe. It appeared he was studying the hem of his coat, fiddling with a loose thread. Greg didn't get the impression he was pouting, but rather that he was deep in thought. Maybe this was the "real" Joe. Not so boisterous and, to put it plainly, immature. This layer beneath the waves of jokes and horny come ons was quiet and contemplative. It was a still pool and Greg desperately wanted to know what fin or claw or tentacle lived within it.

When the train came to a halt, Greg watched as Joe placed his outward mask on again. Could see it unfurl over his face like a veil. He turned to Greg with a smile. "You ready?" he asked, and helped him up. Greg slid his hand in Joe's as they picked their way back up to the surface. He gripped Greg's hand tightly as they ascended, Greek heroes escaping the underworld into the land of the living.

The steps up to the museum were treacherous, but the warmth inside the doors was well worth it. Joe purchased their admissions from the kiosk and it spit out stickers to mark them as paid visitors. Joe slapped it onto Greg's chest, which made him laugh. "What do I owe you?" Greg asked but Joe waved him away, citing his birthday as an excuse for him not to pay.

As they ventured throughout the museum's vaulted ceilinged rooms, it seemed they more or less had the place to themselves. Some of the displays were interactable 3D projections of objects that belonged to other cultures and countries. Joe was enamored with a fossilized raptor skeleton that allowed the viewer to layer on holograms of muscle, then skin, then feathers. He was doing it back and forth, amazed at the detail. It turned Greg's stomach. It felt to Greg like he was watching rotting in reverse.

He chose to focus on a mannequin that projected different ceremonial outfits, with a blurb about each. They all seemed so powerful. He was struck by a figure wearing orange and black, wings extending from their arms, lined with black dots. Greg learned that before their populations dwindled due to climate change, a uniquely colored butterfly called a monarch butterfly was an important part of Día de los Muertos festivities in Mexico. They were viewed as the souls of the dead coming back to visit their loved ones. The imagery could still be seen in traditional celebrations, but the actual butterflies no longer migrated en masse as they once did. What did that mean for the souls, then, he wondered, if humanity had killed off their vessels.

Eventually, Greg was able to peel Joe away from the dead dinosaur and they made unhurried progress through the section. Greg was trying to sneakily shepherd Joe to the painting gallery, as it was his favorite. The majority of pieces were actually digital displays, so they changed quite often, sometimes while you were watching.

Today, the museum was featuring contemporary artists. There were many statement pieces Greg admired. One was an artist's self portrait, at first glance appearing like an old Catholic saint, all goldleaf radiance and billowing clothes. There, the similarities ended, as her face was alive with a sort of manic glee. One hand held a cleaver that was sunk through the opposite arm, the hand of which was holding a crumpled wad of cash, the dark skin laden with legally-distinct company logos. The piece was called "Matthew 5:30".

"I think I get it," Joe said, his head tilted to look at it. "Although I'm not very familiar with Christianity, admittedly."

"I grew up in it," Greg said, admiring the almost photorealism of the piece mixed with the surreal. "Went to church every Sunday until I was a teenager. I can understand the appeal. Jesus made it past

30, and like most people started doing his life's work at that point. Then, he ended up leaving the world anyway, called back up to heaven. So he represents both sides of the big divide. Pretty big deal."

"Do they think God picks who stays and who doesn't?" Joe asked.

"Yeah, they believe God decides everything," Greg said. "It makes some things easier, some things harder." Alissa came to mind. "But from my experience, they don't see it as Him snuffing out lives, but calling them back home, like he did with Jesus." His mother praying, begging, howling like an injured animal. A grief he had no way of comprehending. He must have gone distant, as Joe nudged him gently.

"We don't have to talk about it," Joe said, rubbing Greg's arm.

"That's fine, just thinking," Greg said. They moved on to the next piece. It was one that shifted as you moved around it. A flower blooming and then beginning to wilt until it disappears abruptly. They moved back and forth a few times to get the effect. "I have a question, if it's alright," Greg said. He felt Joe tense a little, but he told Greg to go ahead. "Have you ever been there for someone who didn't make it? Like, you were physically present when it happened?"

"I have," Joe said, not taking his eyes off the artwork. "Have you?"

"No," Greg said. "I was there, but not in the same room." Alcohol-soaked memories, blurs and bits of conversation. Zeke putting him to bed. A hazy image of him standing in the bright doorway, his face obscured by shadow.

"Do you want to talk about it?" Joe asked.

"No, not especially," Greg said and they moved on to the next piece. "But I went down a rabbit hole one night, looking up videos on the internet." He took a deep breath. He wasn't particularly proud of it, and knew it was the kind of thing general society looked down on. But people had posted the recordings and some part of him felt better having seen them. "It seems instantaneous."

"It is," Joe said quietly. "But no need to think about that right now." He stood behind Greg and wrapped his arms around his waist. "I have a question, too," Joe whispered in his ear, pressing himself closer. His breath was warm against the back of Greg's neck, but the chilled spectre of reality brushed against his front, slithering down to his stomach.

They stumbled forward a little, nearly touching the frame. A custodial robot rolled up to them, a fat rounded column on wheels. It chimed and swiveled its circular head towards them, asking them to step further away from the artwork. Joe let go of Greg and they did as the robot requested. It thanked them for patronizing the museum and went about combing the tile floor for debris.

The moment was gone, so they continued on their trek through the selection of modern art. Just before they left the room, there was a piece of a woman, her head resting in an older woman's lap. She was looking out of the frame, tears falling from her sideways face as the older woman sheared her hair away. The piece was titled "Papa". Joe commented that he didn't get it, but Greg did. However melancholy, he was overjoyed to experience his favorite thing about art. He and the woman looking out at him, the artist presumably, were resonating with something similar, across time and space.

A bit morosely, he turned to Joe and told him that going to the museum was an excellent choice for something to do that day. "I'm glad," Joe said and smiled. "Although you don't look too happy right now."

Greg shook his head a little to clear his mind and smiled. "I am, I promise." He checked his phone and dismissed a wave of happy birthday texts and social media posts. One, from his mother, asked for him to call. Greg stared at it for a moment, some beast stunned by the lightspeed approach of a vehicle. He felt Joe at his shoulder again and locked his screen.

"Sorry, didn't mean to pry," Joe said and stepped away.

"You're fine," Greg said, stuffing his phone back into his pocket. "Just checking the time."

"When you're ready, we can go to the next stop," Joe said. "But no rush."

"The next stop? Is it to go get decorations?" Greg asked. Joe gave him a wink and continued walking on, into the sculpture wing of the museum. Along the way, they passed the memorial wall for citizens of the city who didn't make it. Much like the displays in the picture gallery, these shifted from time to time to display different names across the decades. Each one had its own aesthetic theme. The names floated up from the bottom. You could touch the screen and like a river the name would bend around your finger and continue to flow upward. Being called back. Greg pressed his finger onto a name from the previous decade and the letters scattered outward in a starburst before trickling up and away. Maybe that's how easy it was for whatever or whoever made the call. Just drawing names from the bottom of the well. He couldn't bear to look at the next decade's. He might see one of them, a friend or family member. Him.

Joe let out a short psst which got Greg's attention. He motioned for him to catch up and Greg did so, stepping into the area for sculpture exhibits. Amongst the alabaster torsos, wrestling nudes, and breasts covered with gossamer stone, Greg felt his cheeks grow a little warm.

"Are you blushing?" Joe asked incredulously. Greg tried to hide it but that only intensified the heat. They had made their way to an absurd sculpture. A mess of limbs and heads and genitals. It was titled "Friday Night in the Catskills".

"Can I ask you," Greg began, fighting past his initial shock to actually look at the work, "do you sleep with all your clients?" Joe didn't bat a lash, continuing to look at the mix of different materials.

"Would it bother you if I said yes?" Joe asked. "Do you think this is real wood?" he asked, nearly in the same breath, trying to get as close to the structure as he could without touching it or tripping an alarm.

"No, of course not," Greg said, perhaps a little too loud.

"No it's not wood or no it wouldn't bother you?" Joe asked, and Greg could see he was trying to hide a smirk. "I think it is. I've only ever seen it a few times, honestly." Greg was watching him, expectantly, waiting for an answer to his question. "One of my older clients is rich. Stupid rich. Has enough money to choke a goat. His entire house has hardwood floors. And wood furniture. Different kinds of wood too. It's insane."

"I don't want this to sound like a ratty question, but having made it and being that rich...is he just an asshole?" Greg asked. Joe gave him a confused look. "I just mean, someone that has that much going for him would have found someone, right? Gotten married?" Marriage was such a foreign concept to Greg, having only been to one wedding. But he knew plenty of people daydreamed about it. Kept social media collages of inspiration for when the right person and the right time came along.

Greg thought of a couple from his high school that had gotten married the instant they could. It caused a big hubbub. How absurd, he thought to himself. Teenagers in tuxedos. Drinking champagne, which they had just barely become old enough to buy for themselves. Playing dress up and acting so adult. Everyone else he knew had the good sense to wait.

If he made it, though, he'd probably be going to a few within the next few years, for the people his age that also made it. His friend Avni and her girlfriend Trish would probably be getting married before too long.

"I think you're equating wealth with other things that are also deemed markers of success," Joe said, bringing Greg back from his reminiscence. Greg took a moment to process what Joe said, but felt he had been judged severely. "But regardless, what makes you think he's not married?" Joe asked, revolving around the sculpture.

"Oh," Greg's face immediately flashed crimson. "You're like...his secret lover?" Greg asked, scandalized but intrigued.

"No," Joe said, laughing. "Him and his husband hire Ephemeras sometimes. More than one at a time, even." Greg felt the heat radiating off of his face. "It can be lonely having that much money. Not sure who you can trust." Joe had made a full orbit around the piece. "I mean, don't feel bad for him. Again, he's filthy rich." Joe inspected the title card for the sculpture and found that it was, indeed, real wood. "I like it," he said, "because I'm not confused as to my value to him." Greg thought that must be nice, a luxury afforded to few relationships.

"So that's at least one client you've slept with," Greg said, desperately trying to push the conversation back to where it started.

"Oh yeah, I forgot your question." Joe said in a way that clearly indicated he had not forgotten the question. "I'm not sure on exact percentage, so forgive me an estimate, but I'd say it's not as common as you'd think. One person recently just had me help them clean their house and get things organized for if they were gone. The option was there, but they just wanted to make sure it was easy for someone to come get their things."

"Should I do that, you think?" Greg asked. He thought of his little apartment, with its mostly empty cupboards. The closet with two people's clothes. His meager furniture. A pretty sad inventory, all said.

They came to a statue that gave Greg a pit in his stomach for some reason. It was abstract but felt angry and cruel. "You should do what you want to do," Joe said, and made a face at the angry statue. He seemed to be considering it with an ounce of disgust. Perhaps it was one of those pieces that reflected the viewer, somehow, through some unintentional artistic genius of psychology. "I'm sorry if this makes you uncomfortable," he said and then paused, searching for the right words. "But in my mind, if you're gone it won't really matter to you either way if your things are neat or messy." He moved on from the raging lump of clay, but Greg stayed for a little while longer, not quite so repulsed by it the longer he looked.

"I suppose that's true," Greg finally said, but Joe was nowhere near to hear.

The snow had silently started to smother the city while they were safe and warm in the museum. They stopped for a moment after leaving the main entrance to admire the swirling flakes swarming onto signs, congregating in the bike line. A bus crept along the street, its side plastered with an animated ad for Ephemera. A man and woman lounging by a fire that danced and threw warm orange and yellow tones onto the loving pair. Both of them absolutely gorgeous, of course. She was laying against his chest, the model performing some mind-warping yoga flexibility of showing her face in profile and also looking up at him. No one wanted to see the inside of her nostrils, some executive somewhere decided. Her blonde hair cascaded over his reindeer-themed "ugly sweater". His eyes were closed, mid-laugh, as if it were a candid photo. The copy, red and green, read "Don't Spend Another Christmas Alone" with the Ephemera logo, a lowercase e with a heart in its loop. Greg wondered who was supposed to be the client and who was supposed to be the Ephemera in that scenario. Or maybe it was just supposed to be two happy people, to entice an unhappy person to buy what they were peddling. What he had bought.

Greg absent-mindedly dug in his pocket for the pack of cigarettes and fished one out. After a few failed attempts to keep a match's flame alive, Joe was able to light it for Greg. "Such a gentleman," Greg teased. He looked at the end of the cigarette in consideration. "Do you think I should save these for later?" He blew the smoke out of his nose, savoring the smell, the memories it carried. "I always, always wanted to smoke a million cigarettes when I got drunk back in the day."

"Back in the day?" Joe asked.

"At college," Greg said. They started to descend the stairs carefully, watching for ice. Greg was doing his best to follow Joe's lead. However, he didn't really seem to have a destination, and that irked Greg. "We'd all get together to read and critique our pieces and just end up getting drunk and trading sad songs back and forth."

"Sounds like fun," Joe said, and Greg was fairly certain he wasn't being sarcastic.

"They were older for the most part. They did the smart thing and waited until after 30," Greg said. "But I just knew I wanted to make movies, and I figured college would be the place to do that."

"Did you ever get someone to let you film them sleep, fry eggs in the nude, things like that?" Joe asked. "I can see it, young Greg constantly surveying the scene," he said and held his fingers to form a rectangle.

"That was me," Greg said, and had the idea to loop his arm through Joe's. He worked up the nerve and did so, Joe clasping his arm naturally. "I wanted to make something important at some point," Greg said, "and if not important, at least good."

"Did you ever do that?" Joe asked and led him around a corner.

"I've got a couple of shorts I put together," Greg said. "But after college I had to earn a living, so I haven't even thought about making a film for fun in a long time." Joe mentioned he'd like to see Greg's shorts and Greg felt himself turn crimson at the mere thought of showing them to another living person.

"Did you at least make videos for your job you have 'slash' had?" Joe asked.

"Kind of. I mostly just did the work around commercials. Provided a few ideas, but it was a lot of spreadsheets and emails, mostly. Other people got to go film and edit them."

Joe took an abrupt turn down an alleyway, which zigged and zagged a few times. Greg was amazed to see that there was a tiny marketplace nestled among the buildings. Just a few shops, it looked like, but they had hung up twinkling fairy lights and made it look very charming. The whole thing felt like he had stumbled into a different world.

"Next stop," Joe said and gestured to a storefront. It had pink and blue neon buzzing out onto the glass, spelling out "Wild World". Greg used up the last bit of the cigarette and flicked it out into the snow, where it disappeared.

"If this is a strip club-" Greg began, but Joe tugged him

forward, into the door.

Inside was dimly lit, but scored with neon of every color. Synth-heavy muzak was playing overhead. The room itself was littered with smaller rooms that had sliding glass doors, above which were arranged a series of lights that seemed familiar to Greg. A screen to the right of the door showed the Wild World logo. As they peeled off their coats and scarves, one of the room's lights switched from red to green and the door slid open. Three or four people clambered out, laughing hysterically. Before the door slid shut, Greg saw the walls of the room looked like an obstacle course with absurd colors.

"Wait...is this a holoroom arcade?" Greg asked and Joe grinned. "I had no idea we had one in the city." Greg couldn't help but smile. "I always wanted to try but my mom wouldn't let me and then they all went out of business when I was still a kid."

"This one apparently was a sex shop for a while, which kept it afloat. But they kept the holorooms. And now people are interested in them again." Joe walked up to the now empty room and touched the screen. The Wild World logo was replaced by a selection screen. "What'll you have?" Joe asked. The screen had such offerings as "Dino Safari", "Manor of the Zombies", and "Escape From Future Robot Bounty Hunter II". Greg was tickled by their cheesiness. "We can play whichever one you want," Joe said, waving his phone over the pay pad. Just below it was an old-fashioned coin slot, and beside it its brother, a bill reader. Both were dead and dark, merely part of the room's exoskeleton now.

"Isn't it crazy people used to carry physical money around?"

Greg mused. "How gross is that? Just carrying slivers of metal coated in other people's germs. Just a waste of good metal."

"I think you're focusing on the wrong thing," Joe said with a patient smile. "What if there's still some naughty ones on here," he leaned in and whispered to Greg. "'Night of the Leather Witch' or something like that." Greg told him to shush, he couldn't concentrate. Greg scrolled through the selections and started to feel the grip of choice paralysis. He closed his eyes and picked "Kaiju Defense Go!". The door slid open and welcomed them inside, closing behind them. The Wild World logo was lazily drifting across rainbow colored walls, bouncing each time it hit an edge.

The walls began to fade to black, Greg and Joe barely able to see each other. A screeching cry pierced the darkness and the walls faded into a city skyline. Giant insects swarmed in the distance, beginning to circle around them. "What do we do?" Greg yelled over the drone of their enormous wings.

"Hell if I know!" Joe called back. "Uh, Holoroom. Instructions?" he asked but it made no sound of recognition. One of the insects slammed into the wall closest to Greg and he nearly jumped out of his skin. Joe laughed and Greg gave the bug the finger. A radiant pink laser beam shot from a point in the screen and pierced a nearby building. "-500" in bold red block numbers floated up from the smoking puncture wound. Greg experimentally pointed at a bug above them and the laser beam shot through its abdomen. It exploded into green and purple fireworks and a gold "+100" danced on the screen for a moment. Joe caught on and soon they were blasting bugs at a fever pitch.

Before he knew it, Greg was having a hard time moving he was laughing so hard. They fell into a kind of groove after a few levels, calling out weak spots to one another. After 50 levels, they fought the boss, which was a chimeric creature, blending centipede, beetle, and praying mantis. In the end, Greg's arms burning and his shirt drenched with sweat, they defeated the alien bug queen and the walls danced with congratulatory "HI SCORE"s.

The door slid open again and the cityscape on the walls faded back to black. Beneath the selection screen, a thin plastic ticket reading "PRIZE" shot out. Taking it to the prize counter, they fed the ticket into a claw machine, which jerked to life and grabbed their reward: a small plush of one of the alien beetles from the game.

"Our child," Greg said.

"I'm not ready to be a father," Joe said, laughing.

"I'll raise him on my own then," Greg said, holding the bug close to his chest.

"Did you work off breakfast?" Joe asked. Greg realized he was actually pretty hungry. He checked his phone and saw they had spent two hours in the room. He had more birthday texts. His more sentimental friends waxed poetic. They wished him well. They thanked him for the memories and told him not to worry. He paused at one from Peter.

"Dropped off your present in your mail box. Hope it's a good day."

"Ready to grab lunch? There's a great little cafe next door."

They grabbed their coats and darted out into the cold and into the next shop. Greg immediately took in the great smells of coffee and baking bread. Looking around the shop he stopped, surprised to see a familiar face.

"Avni?" he asked and she waved happily.

"Surprise!" she said and got up to hug him. "Joe reached out and scheduled a little lunch for us."

"Wow," Greg said. He was happy to see Avni but he had also intentionally made it so he wouldn't see anyone from his normal life during the day. He had planned on billing Joe as a recent dating prospect. But he guessed there was no hope in that anymore. Joe seemed to evaporate, now standing at the counter ordering for them. Greg took a seat at her table, placing the bug plush in the middle. She took his hands in hers.

"How are you feeling?" she asked, "And no bullshit."

"We've had a really good day," Greg said and smiled. "Breakfast, the museum, the arcade."

"You can thank me for the museum," Avni said. "But you didn't answer my question."

"Well, to be honest, I'm freaked out," Greg said. "I'm a time bomb and there's no way of knowing if it's a dud or not."

"I understand," she said with pity. "You remember my party. I was such a mess." She let his hands go to get her coffee cup and take a sip. "But life is always uncertain, birthday or no. There's nothing to say you won't get hit by a bus on the way home, you know?" She looked in his eyes and nearly dropped her coffee. "Oh my God, I'm sorry. What a stupid thing to say."

"You're fine," he said. Mercifully, Joe had returned, placing an iced latte down in front of Greg, along with an enormous cinnamon bun. "Even if I make it, I think Joe's trying to give me diabetes," Greg said. "French toast this morning, now this."

"You're welcome, I guess," Joe said and stuck out his tongue. "You're crazy for drinking iced drinks in the winter."

"Listen, if there was ever a day to eat guilt free, it would be today," Avni said and Joe agreed. "Have you talked to your mom?"

"We said goodbye yesterday," Greg said, tearing off a piece of the cinnamon roll.

"What's that mean?" Avni asked.

"What I said. We said goodbye yesterday." She was clearly waiting for more information and his bite of cinnamon bun only lasted so long. "I told her not to come to the party," Greg said, barely more than a whisper. Joe and Avni shared a look, which Greg didn't appreciate. How long had they been in contact, anyway?

"It's your birthday, do what you want," she said, and Greg felt the weight of the impending "but". "But don't you think she wants to be there?" Avni asked.

"Maybe, but I don't want her to be," Greg said and shrugged.

"This may not be the best time to say so," Avni said, "But I won't be there either." Greg looked at her, trying not to accuse her of betrayal. She winced apologetically. "Me and Trish are catching the train tonight. They have some big Christmas thing for her company out at the boss's mansion. Everyone's staying the night. She's pretty positive she's getting that promotion."

"Gotcha," Greg said. "Well, then I appreciate you taking the time to see me today before you left," he said. How mature, how very stable, he thought to himself.

"Andy?" someone was standing at their table now, their hand on Joe's shoulder. "I'm so sorry to interrupt, but I had to come say hi." Joe looked at Greg for a fleeting moment then stood and hugged the stranger.

"You look good," Joe said, sitting back down.

"Thanks, man," the stranger said. "Just got married over the summer. There's my wife, now." They waved at a woman entering the shop, pulling a knit cap off her hair, which danced up into the air on static. She smiled and came over to the table. "Sara, this is Andy. Remember, I told you all about him." The awkward pain behind Sara's smile seemed obvious to everyone but her spouse. "Are you still doing the Ephemera thing?" they asked.

"Uh, yeah," Joe said and reflexively looked to Greg again. "It's Greg's birthday, actually. 30 today."

"Oh man, now I feel even worse for interrupting. I'm such an idiot," the stranger said and extended a hand. Greg took it. "Good luck on your birthday! I won't take up any more of your time." They turned to Andy again. Placed their hand on his shoulder again. "Andy, you've got my number. Give me a shout sometime." Joe and Sara looked at one another briefly, saying it was nice to meet each other, before they left to go order their drinks. Greg felt a slight satisfaction in Joe taking a turn being the one to blush. But not enough to completely quell his agitation.

"Andy, huh," Greg said, rattling the ice in his drink.

"Does that surprise you?" Joe, or was it Andy, said, on the defensive.

"Avni, you were just saying how Trish might get that promotion. How's everything on your end?" Greg asked, willing himself not to look at Joe for the rest of the conversation. He hated himself a little for talking about work. That's all anyone talked about. They didn't make small talk, they weren't those friends. Avni graciously took the conversation topic and went with it. She was a teacher and her kids were ecstatic about the holidays. They had typed emails to Santa and attached doodles they'd done on their displays. She showed Greg a few on her phone.

"What about you? You never told me how your good luck party at work went," Avni said.

"Horrendous," Greg said, leaning back in his chair. He relayed it all to her, embellishing a little bit. Avni couldn't stop laughing at the cake and what an utter disaster the whole thing was. By the end of it, they were turning heads, getting loud. "If nothing else," Greg said, "I don't think I'm gonna go back there, whether I make it or not."

"Well, you shouldn't have to. To them that was an under 30 job and they paid you what they thought was enough. Which was insulting, I'm sure." Avni sighed and took another drink. "What about Peter, though?"

"Peter?" Joe finally chimed in.

"What about Peter?" Greg asked and took another chunk out

of the cinnamon bun. "We don't have to work together to be friends."

"No, of course not. But you won't have the coffee break chats or get to commiserate over what's her face in accounting." Greg shrugged. "Is he coming to the party?"

Greg glanced at Joe. "He said he was the last time I saw him. He texted that he had left a present for me back at the apartment, though."

"Aw, how sweet," Avni said.

"I'm taking it you have a little crush on Peter?" Joe asked.

"Oh God, a crush?" Greg asked, rolling his eyes, but wanting to keep Joe feeling jealous. "I'm 30, dammit." Avni's phone chimed.

"It's Trish. I still have to pack for the trip and you know it's giving her fits." Her eyes darted over the text and she sent a reply quickly. "I should probably be heading on. But let's hang out next week." She started putting her coat back on.

"If-" Greg began.

"Next week," she said firmly and kissed him on the cheek. "Oh, before I forget," she said and pulled a tube of lipstick out of her coat pocket. "For good luck." The lipstick was a deep, almost violent red. "I wore it at my party."

"I remember that," Greg said and smiled sadly. "We all had red lip prints all over our faces after midnight." He hugged Avni tightly, squeezing as hard as he could. She did the same. Greg refused to be the first to let go. When they finally parted, they both had tears welling in their eyes. She eventually left and as Greg watched her back, he thought of a million other things he wanted to talk to her about. If she had seen any good movies recently. What had really pissed her off in the last few days. If she was happy now that she was on the other side of 30.

He sat with Joe in silence for a moment, wiping the tears away with the back of his hand. "I'm 2 and 0 for crying jags today, I guess," Greg said.

"Stop feeling bad about it," Joe said pointedly. "No one should judge you for it, especially yourself." He placed his hand on top of Greg's. Greg tried to wait long enough that it didn't seem obvious, but he withdrew his hand after a few moments and picked at the cinnamon bun. "Say whatever's on your mind," Joe said levelly. "It's pointless for you to waste any time being sullen."

"Well," Greg said and hazarded a glance at Joe. "Doesn't it just 'serve to ruin the illusion' to bring all your clients to the same place?"

"Believe it or not," Joe said, "there is such a thing as coincidence. I haven't seen that person in two years. This place is hard to find, but it's also not invisible."

Greg sighed. "Regardless, what about your name? I know 'Joe' is a fake now. Fake just like everything else about this I guess." He pushed his plate away from him a little, severely wanting the last bit of pastry but trying to prove a point. He was pouting. But what was that old song his grandpa sang about crying at your own party?

Joe ran his finger along the lip of his coffee mug and thought for a moment. "Would you consider there's a reason for that?" Greg raised an eyebrow, telling him to go on. Joe lowered his voice a little and leaned closer. "This isn't always a happy job and it isn't always a safe one. It is legal, but that doesn't mean things don't go sideways." Greg began to return his gaze to the crumb-laden plate, but Joe nudged him to bring Greg's eyes back to his face. "Right now, this might be your last day on earth and you're handling it a certain way. It occurs to me you're prone to highs and lows on a normal day." Greg felt a hot knot of anger forming in his throat. "But while that comes out of you as sulking, maybe throwing little sassy barbs my way, other people don't want to go out alone. Others, if they make it, are so happy and they make something more out of what I am to them."

"Isn't that a little bit of your own fault?" Greg asked, and for the second time patrons turned to look at him. Lowering his voice again, he said, "You get paid to fake intimacy with people. Do you hope they don't make it? So you don't have to worry about them being 'clingy' after you've spent however long with them?" He was making this all so much harder than it had to be. He could just keep his mouth shut. He could be reasonable and just drop it. Instead, he said, "You just use lonely people to get your cash and then you want to disappear. Clean break. Gone forever?" He had poked an accusing finger into Joe's chest at the end of his diatribe. Joe stared at Greg for a small eternity, obvious anger in his furrowed brow and flared nostrils.

"It's a two way street, I promise you that." Joe stood and began to put on his jacket.

"Where are you going?" Greg asked, standing too.

"We've got somewhere to be," Joe said, pulling the zipper up to his chin.

"Are we going to act like that didn't just happen?" Greg said, putting on his own coat, disarmed by Joe's passivity.

"You wanted to know about my job, and at this point I think you might actually want to make yourself a little more miserable, so I'll let you have it." Joe pushed his chair in. "Yes, we are going to move forward with the day. And I'm going to tell you this: we have less than 12 hours to go together. At the end of that, you being mad or sad or any of those things won't matter to me." He picked up the bug plush and shoved it into Greg's chest. "But right now, I'm on the clock. So I am going to do everything I'm supposed to to make you happy." He began to walk away, and turned back to say, "Grab your scarf and let's go."

"My scarf?" Greg asked.

"Yes, you left the house with a scarf. Red, frayed at the ends." Joe's anger had already ebbed away, or else he was very good at shoving it down. Greg's hand went to his neck. Zeke's scarf. He didn't bring it to the cafe. The realization settled on him as a cold chill.

"Oh my God," Greg said and piled out of the cafe. He dashed back to the arcade and began looking about frantically. He checked the room they had used, which was still empty. Joe came in behind him as he made his way to the prize counter. "Hello? Hello! Are there any humans here?" he shouted.

"Hey, what's the matter?" Joe asked, trying to grab Greg's shoulder. Greg pulled away from his hand and knocked on the counter's glass case. "Someone may have grabbed it by accident. Or a cold homeless person is making good use of it." Tears began to streak down Greg's cheeks. "It's okay!" Joe said in a coddling way. "It sucks to lose something but I can get you a new one."

"Shut up," Greg said sternly and dried his tears. "Are there seriously no fucking people here?" he started to say to Joe but it turned into a yell into the space in general.

"Honestly, probably not. It's mostly automated I think." Joe peered around the room, but didn't see anyone, employee or otherwise. "Was it important to you?" he asked, "Sentimental to someone?"

"You wouldn't get it," Greg said, defeated. It was just a scarf, he knew. He was acting like a lunatic, he knew that as well. "Let's just go get these decorations or whatever else bullshit you've got cooked up." He left the arcade but quickly realized he had no idea where they were meant to go. So he waited for a minute in the cold. The snow had lost its magic in his mind. It was freezing now, trying to claim his fingers and toes. It stung his ears and nose. He stared up into the red-gray clouds, the falling snow like stars flying by at hyperspeed. The cold air bit at his lungs, but it also served to cool him down emotionally. The bright white heat of his embarrassment, his guilt, his shame, burned itself out as he took deep breaths.

Joe finally exited the building. "Sorry, I went through and checked every room and found an employee after all. They didn't have anything in the lost and found, so someone must have grabbed it." Greg nodded solemnly. Joe offered Greg open arms and Greg accepted the embrace. Joe squeezed him tightly.

"Sorry," Greg said and Joe shushed him quietly, rocking slightly. "Today's just been a bit of a roller coaster already," he said, sniffling into Joe's coat.

"You're telling me," Joe said with a chuckle. "We'll get everything done and get home so you can relax before people start showing up. I'll rub your feet and everything." Home he said, as if it were his own.

Greg swallowed a lump in his throat. "And I'm sorry for what I said about your job. I don't really think you take advantage-"

"Water under the bridge," Joe said and let Greg go. "If you're ready, let's go to our next stop. Then we'll get the stuff for the party. There's a store right on the way." He started walking back down the alleyway before Greg could say anything else. They walked in silence for a while, dodging snow plow robots with wide tank tread clacking down the sidewalk. Ghosts of Christmas carols drifted out of stores as they passed, whispers on the wind that blustered around them. Eventually, Greg had to fall in line behind Joe, who was tailing a plow. He watched Joe's back as the snow made him look further and further away, no matter how much Greg tried to keep up.

Greg realized where they were headed when they got a few blocks away. He had made this trek many times. They rounded a corner and Greg saw it. A faded metal sign with chipped paint housed blinking bulbs that spelled out the word "CALIGARI". The sign was an arrow pointing down to the door. His stomach did a sick somersault. Joe opened the door and Greg swore it was just the same way Zeke did it. Maybe there were just so many ways to open doors and hold them open for people. Greg stepped into a small, square lobby with red, raggedy carpet that was peppered with maroon splotches. Like pools of blood.

The place had a smell that he thought he had forgotten. But being there, he realized it had never left its little burrow in the back of his mind. It just smelled old. A basement and somehow an attic at the same time. Over it all was the mouthwatering smell of popcorn.

"Hey there, stranger," the owner, Mr. Caligari said to Greg from the ticket booth concession stand.

"Oh, you've been here?" Joe asked. Greg couldn't tell if he was disappointed it wasn't as much of a surprise or if he would just be annoyed by anything Greg did at this point. "Guess I should have known, being a film nut." Greg greeted Mr. Caligari and they caught up. Business had been slow, but it had been slow for the last 20 years he'd owned it. He was convinced some higher power just made it all work. Mr. Caligari said he had a place to sleep, food to eat, and got to share movies with people. He was happy.

When it became Greg's turn to provide his half of the catching up conversation, he felt itchy, uncomfortable. Mr. Caligari told him not to worry, it wasn't his business why Greg and the other fella he came in with called it quits. He remarked how handsome Joe was and told Greg he was a keeper. "I just feel it," he said.

"It's my birthday," Greg said, trying to change the subject. Mr. Caligari pantomimed a heart attack, gripping his chest.

"Well! Is it the big one?" he asked, his eyes bright and alive beneath their heavy leads. Greg told him that it was indeed his 30th. Mr. Caligari clapped his hands and said everything was on the house. He got them some sugary drinks and two enormous tubs of popcorn.

"If I may, I have just the thing. You'll love it." Greg thanked him. "Don't worry about it. Good luck to you," he said and ushered them through a red door to his left.

Inside was a long hallway, the blood splotch carpet oozing under the door and down to the furthest wall. Along its length were rooms with bulbs above them, much like the holoroom arcade. Greg guessed this was the blueprint the arcades built off of. The green lights buzzed, some flickering as they walked. The light above the room at the very end of the hall switched to red as they approached. Greg opened the door and stepped into a small room with a sofa. A projector clung to the ceiling, spraying out a cone of white light onto the wall opposite the door.

Joe seemed a little confused. "I thought movie theaters were, I don't know, big rooms with lots of chairs."

"They were a long time ago," Greg said, setting his popcorn and drink down on a small table on one end of the sofa so he could take his jacket off. "And in some places they've started doing it that way again. A while back, this weird flu caused a bunch of them to shut down, since people couldn't be close to strangers for risk of spreading it. So they adapted to more private viewing experiences." Greg had set his food down as well. Joe marveled at his film knowledge, but was sure it was feigned.

"People definitely fool around in these, right?" Joe asked. He pulled his coat off and draped it over an arm of the sofa.

"I have," Greg said flatly. He was just as surprised as Joe hearing the words leave his mouth. A few flashes of him and Zeke ignoring whatever classic they had paid to watch in another of these rooms. Trying hard to be quiet. Hearing people in the room next to theirs.

"Is that so?" Joe said, smiling, his teeth flashing in the dark. Greg felt a little relief. He wanted Joe to like him. Wanted to impress him. The vulnerable, belly presenting desperation for the approval of a guy that had made him unable to start another relationship. "The 'other guy' the old man was talking about, maybe?" Joe asked, sliding down onto the couch.

"That's right," Greg said, tossing some popcorn in his mouth. He took the time he was chewing to figure out how he would word this properly. What details he could be vague on, maybe tweak a little to keep him from connecting the dots. A scarf worth a nervous breakdown, his empty apartment, the human-shaped hole he kept dancing around. "An old boyfriend," he said, settling on a hand-waving gesture. Not important enough to talk about. But important enough to change the entire course of his life.

"Bad memories?" Joe asked in an exaggeratedly sultry voice. "We can make some new ones." Greg shushed him as the projector clicked and the white light turned to black and white and gray. "Disappeared!" was the movie's title, spelled out in tall block letters. Joe reached out and dug in his coat pocket. First, he grabbed the bug plush from the arcade and planted it on Greg's shoulder. Greg had forgotten about their child in the flurry of losing the scarf, but was happy Joe had remembered it. "Cuddle up with that," he said, digging around for something else. Eventually, he pulled out two pills, holding them out on his palm. "Want one?"

"What's that?" Greg asked, trying to pay attention to the opening. A woman with a transatlantic accent talking on a rotary phone, cold and statuesque.

"A mild hallucinogen," Joe said. "It doesn't last very long, but it's great for watching movies. And it makes everything taste amazing." He popped one in his mouth and washed it down with some soda. "No pressure. I just remember it being on your list."

The list. He was such an idiot. When he filled it out, he had listed that he'd never done anything other than tobacco, weed, and alcohol. Those were the legal things, the ones no one really batted an eye at. Greg most certainly didn't want to do something that would make his heart explode or cause his dick to shoot off like a rocket. "What if I have a bad trip?" Greg asked. His achilles heel, the cowardice in him. He was so afraid of what his mind might conjure. It seemed to do a pretty good job on its own filling the shadows with leering eyes and leaning figures.

"You won't if you don't think about it," Joe said, sinking down into the cushions. Greg countered it may have an adverse effect with his other medications. Joe said he had already done research and there were no bad reactions with what he was taking. In fact, it was being used to treat depression in some trials. "Here," he put the pill into Greg's hand. "Take it if you want, don't if you don't."

Greg held the pill between his fingers. He took pills every morning, every night. During the day, if he was already feeling particularly dark. What was one more? Without thinking too much he popped it into his mouth and took a gulp of soda. He watched as the stern woman on the telephone absent-mindedly kissed her wife's cheek as she left for work. Her whole attitude had changed. Don't forget, she said, her party started at 7. When her wife had left, she informed whoever she was talking to of this fact. Some clandestine plan was coming together. Joe's hand floated over on top of Greg's. Their fingers interlaced.

Sinking further into the couch, Greg felt he was drifting downward, the ground nowhere to be seen. But it wasn't a freefall, not a panicked wailing comet burning through the atmosphere. It was gentle. He was a feather, floating down the stream. Merrily, merrily, merrily, merrily. Greg felt his whole body hum. The movie kept going, but he had lost the plot. He was okay with that. The people were beautiful and it made him nostalgic for a time he never knew, and probably never existed.

Greg felt a slight squirming against his arm. He lifted it to realize he had leaned down on top of the beetle. It slowly twitched its soft felt legs, life coursing through them. Eventually, it was able to clasp onto Greg's arm. It climbed up to his chest and rested there, its pincers slowly spreading and closing. Greg stroked its fuzzy carapace and it clicked happily. What a beautiful family they were. Dad, father, and beetle baby. Greg would have to be the disciplinarian, he knew. Joe would be good cop. Maybe that was for the best.

He idly envied the beetle and its simplicity. Just living its life by impulse, imperative. Writhe around in the dirt and eat enough and wait long enough for your entire body to change. Emerge from the earth with enough life to reproduce and die a clean death. Just months of life and the ability to accomplish everything your body told you must be done. Maybe that's what 30 was. He would no longer have this squishy grub body. He'd be made into something beautiful.

Greg wasn't sure how much time had passed, but he eventually found his attention drifting back to the projected picture.

The main character in the movie was looking both ways before crossing the street. She was wearing dark glasses and a sheer scarf wrapped around her hair. The height of espionage disguise. People walked on either side of the street, got into cars that would likely be their demise. Greg wanted to tell them not to do it. Warn them that all it took was a single tire in the wrong lane.

A man was talking behind the main character and her liaison as they spoke. Greg's heart began to pound. One of the people in the background was Greg. The other was Zeke. Zeke kept turning to look at the Greg on the couch with Joe, then back to the Greg in the movie. He was gesturing towards real Greg. Accusatory. Angry. He began walking towards the camera, growing larger. Kept drawing closer until he pushed through the conversation in the foreground, the characters cursing at him. The wall was nothing but his face. He was furious, brows knitted. The way Greg had only seen him maybe once or twice. The beetle pinched Greg then, on his neck. He screamed, jumping up and raking at his skin.

Joe was looking up at him from the couch, bewildered. "I'm sorry," Joe said. "I didn't mean to scare you." The beetle plush was laying on the couch, lifeless. Greg took a shuddering breath. He slowly turned to face the wall again, a tear evaporating into a steam-filled soap bubble on his cheek, oil-slick iridescent. He didn't want to look. But he had to. Had to make himself endure Zeke's righteous anger.

But the movie was back to normal. The woman returned to her car and eased it out into traffic. Greg sat back down, taking a drink of his soda, breathing heavy. "Can I try again?" Joe asked. His eyes were half shut, somewhere between dreaming and waking. Greg sat back and Joe kissed his neck where the beetle had bitten him. He felt a tingle radiate from where Joe's lips touched his skin, seemed to yank all his nerves in that direction. More of that. Don't stop. Greg turned his face and placed his lips on Joe's. He tasted like popcorn. Grease and salt. Joe's tongue came roving over Greg's teeth.

In the movie, a gunshot went off and it caused Greg to start and pull away. He wiped his mouth with the back of his hand and fell back into the cushions. Joe sat up and leaned away onto the arm rest of the sofa. He probably thought Greg was reacting to the kiss. Greg started to babble, explaining why it wasn't Joe but Greg was getting frustrated that the film wouldn't stay still, that the wallpaper patterns kept dancing. He was really enjoying their time together. Greg worried that he was being too much or too little. Even if he was paying for Joe to be there with him in this moment, he still wanted him to enjoy it. Hated the thought of Joe biding his time, watching the countdown until it reached 0. Joe had walked into a house of cards mid-collapse. Degradation and crumbling from the top down. Most of all, Greg just wanted to be happy. And isn't that all anybody really wanted? He asked Joe if that's all he wanted, too.

He looked to Joe for a response, but realized he hadn't said any of it out loud. Too much of a hassle now to try and say it again. Greg stood up and walked behind the sofa to the door. The knob turned before his hand touched it. The door swung open slowly. The red hallway bent and twisted, like the throat of some giant beast. The floor was now the ceiling and Greg was walking on it, his shirt pulled down to his armpits. The age old blood in the carpets started to drip out and the beast shuddered with every step he took. He felt its pulse as he held onto the nearest door frame. Ants poured out from under his palms, marching off in orderly lines to find spilled soda and popcorn chunks.

The doors along the hallway were ajar. Greg couldn't resist peeking into the closest one, pulling himself forward on the door frame. Sweat and wet mouths. Convulsions. Tortured breaths and holy worship of flesh and spit. He started to gag and a torrent of pills poured out and upward onto the floor. A few clung to his bottom lip as he tried to catch his breath. They tasted of chalk and self-doubt. "Do you mind?" the main character from the movie was hanging her head out of the nearby open door. Her gray skin seemed grainy and jumped to the left for a brief moment, revealing a white spot of nothing. He asked her what was going on. Her mouth opened wide and made the sound of a shocked inhale, a thousand people gasping as they saw fire in the sky.

He blinked and he was in the room with Joe again. In the movie, the woman's wife was confronting her. But Zeke's voice came out of her mouth. Why did she lie? The woman turned and it was Greg in the dark shades and the scarf wrapped around his hair. He held a pistol shakily in his gloved hand. He asked Zeke why shouldn't he be able to take advantage of his 30th? He could just leave it all behind. Let everyone believe he was dead. He could start over, didn't Zeke get that? He wouldn't owe anyone anything. All the dead people hanging over him would lose the scent and stop hounding him. He was clutching at his face now, mascara running down his cheeks, lipstick smeared, streaked to his chin. Zeke could only look on with disgust, the cigarette in his fingers smoldering, his smart pantsuit helping him blend into the shadows of the room. Zeke finished the cigarette and flicked the butt at Greg, who was crumpled on the floor, clutching the gun to his chest. Before Zeke left, he told Greg he might as well leave. Anyone who wanted to be gone that badly shouldn't stick around.

Greg grabbed a handful of popcorn and shoved it into his mouth. It was truly incredible.

The credits began to roll and Joe stirred from his spot. Dim lighting rose from the floor so they could see to collect their things but not be struck blind. When the movie ended, so did Greg's high, more or less. He felt tired. A shirt beaten on a river rock and left out to dry. "Well?" Joe asked, standing up and stretching. "What did you think?"

"I think I don't want to take hallucinogens ever again," Greg said. He put on his coat and stuffed the plush down into its interior pocket. The trip hadn't been all bad, he guessed.

"You seemed to be having a good time," Joe said, putting on his own coat. Greg asked what Joe meant as he collected their garbage. Joe gave him a weird look but shrugged it off. "You were laughing the last half of the movie," he said. "After the gunshot startled you."

"After you kissed me?" Greg asked. "That happened, right?"

"It did," Joe said. "You seemed to like that too." He came closer, pulling the zipper of Greg's coat up a little higher, pulling him forward slightly. Greg blushed and cleared his throat. Joe didn't push it. Instead he opened the door to the hallway. No porno sounds or dripping carpet.

Even so, Greg kept his head down as they walked down the hall, dragging his hand along the wall so he'd know if it started to shift again. Luckily, it stayed put. The beast was sleeping once more. Back in the lobby, Mr. Caligari asked how Greg enjoyed the movie. He lied and said he loved it. Maybe he would have loved it, if he had watched it at all. Mr. Caligari said he had plenty more like it for the next time they came in. Greg thanked him, wanting to just be out in the cold air.

"What did you see when you tripped?" Greg asked as they crossed the street. He assumed they were headed to pick up the party supplies but didn't really care at this point. His mouth was dry and felt gritty.

"Just wavy lines and shimmery textures. What'd you see?" Joe asked.

"Same thing," Greg said, tucking his face into the collar of his coat. "Just wanted to make sure that was normal."

Greg lost track of time for a while, feeling like his soul was drifting out of sync with his body. He just kept walking. If he just kept walking, they'd end up where they were going. At one point, they passed a store display that caught his attention, so they stopped. There were people in their underwear, posing like mannequins in the store window. The longer Greg looked, the more he became uncomfortable, noticing the dullness of their eyes. He looked closer and could swear he saw seams along their fingers and wrists.

"Let's go in," Joe said, and before Greg could object they were inside. Some light piano music was playing from the ceiling. It looked like they had walked into a well-lit, poshly decorated slaughterhouse. Legs, arms, breasts, pieces of people were categorized and shelved by skin color.

"Welcome!" a sales associate said from the back of the store. His coworker kept talking and he shushed them. He swept some christmas cookie crumbs off his shirt and came up to them. "How can I help you today?"

"We actually just didn't know what this...was?" Joe said and gestured around.

"Oh! We are a Custom Companion retailer," the sales representative said and did an equally sweeping gesture. "You can assemble the perfect person just for you. Sexually or otherwise." Greg looked up at the ceiling then, already feeling his cheeks growing hot.

"I've read about these," Joe said, and Greg wasn't sure if he was faking it. "Apparently Ephemera has a deal with you all?"

"That's right! You can 'rent' a Custom Companion through Ephemera. And I can assure you, they are thoroughly sanitized." Kyle looked Joe up and down.

"We may just do that," Joe said, giving a thumbs up to Greg, who was trying really hard not to look as murderous as he felt.

"If you try it out and like it, you absolutely should get one for yourselves. Spice things up a little bit!" Kyle said, not even pretending to give Greg a second glance. "And not to worry, I tell everyone first thing, there are payment plans, so don't let all the sticker prices here in the store scare you off."

"Can we see the penises?" Joe asked. Greg reached out and punched him.

"Of course! Right over there on the wall," he said and pointed to the selection. "Our higher end models are customizable after completion, so you don't have to necessarily narrow it down to one option." Greg caught the sales person winking at Joe and Joe smirking back. He felt himself turning sullen. "I'll leave you two to look around. My name is Kyle. Just give me a shout if you need anything. You may actually have to shout," he said, laughing fakely. Kyle grabbed onto Joe's arm as he laughed, tossing his head back. "We're in the back eating too many sweets and watching Drummond House."

"Oh! My husband Larry loves Drummond House," Joe said, pointing at Greg.

"Have you watched the finale?" Kyle asked, finally deigning to look in his direction.

"Started it, but didn't get to finish," Greg said, giving Joe a look.

"Okay, we won't ruin anything. Promise," Kyle said and retreated to the back of the store.

Joe looked at Greg, trying not to burst out in laughter. "Wow," Greg said quietly. "You suck," he said, smacking Joe's arm. "Also, Larry?" Greg asked, offended. Joe laughed and meandered around to an endcap display of different lips. "This place is so creepy," Greg said. A nearby arm grazed him and he nearly jumped out of his skin. It felt like the hand was gripping onto his coat. Joe ran a finger from one end to the other.

This was not the place to be coming down from a bad trip.

"It's crazy, feel it," Joe said. Greg made a face but Joe grabbed his hand and put it on the arm. It definitely felt like skin. Or something like it. Greg yanked his hand back and tried to shake off the sensation. "I just don't get it," Greg said, examining a leg that was covered in curly hair.

"You sure?" Joe asked, pointing to himself. He thought of the empty bed nights. The nights that he didn't have an empty bed but didn't feel any better. Failed connections and lackluster hookups.

"Okay, so I get it," Greg said, "needing companionship. And maybe for under 30's it could be a surrogate instead of being tied down." He went up to a kiosk nearby that displayed what was a lot like a character builder in a video game. He cycled through different heads and torsos. "But imagine, you don't make it. What's your mom gonna do with your...sex bot?" There was a second screen with personality quirks and sliders. "It looks like they have AI options," Greg said. "I bet people make some real Frankenstein's monsters out of these things."

"You're getting into it," Joe said, picking up one of the arms and running it down Greg's leg.

"Ew, you sicko," Greg said, smacking the arm away. He regretted it, instantly thinking of how much that single part probably cost. "Seriously, what does that look like? You get this, 'Custom Companion', but you don't finish the payments before you go so now not only does your mom have to figure out how to live with your sex bot, but she's gotta pay it off too. Surely they don't do refunds or returns."

"You know my stance on it," Joe said, putting the arm back on its rack. If you're not around to know, who cares, he meant. "That may be how Ephemera gets theirs to rent out, come to think of it." Greg thought this made sense.

"Do you think the 'robot's gonna take your job'?" Greg asked. He remembered these sentiments from his mom and some other older family members. Young people didn't know how to work. Had to leave it to robots that couldn't even be called bird-brained. How would these kids ever learn anything about suffering if they didn't have to get their hands dirty. As if the world wasn't passing around suffering by the handful.

"Nah, it's hard to beat the real deal," Joe said and flexed his bicep. Greg made a gagging face and rolled his eyes. "But I am glad it's an option for people. Probably lower risk of STIs, if they are sanitized as well as Kyle said they were. No pregnancy scares." He spun a head on its lazy susan display and pointed to a small hole at the base of its skull, surrounded by concentric dull gray circles. "What's this?"

"I think that's a charger port," Greg said, examining the 3D model on the screen. The product description mentioned fast charging. He expanded the window to see a block of fine print. The 'Custom Companion's' 'Human Companion(s)' must insert plug firmly until it clicks. Custom Companions are unable to plug in their own cables. Custom Companions only operate within a certain radius of their charging station. "Do you think people…you know?" Joe asked, sliding his finger towards the charging port.

"Good lord," Greg said.

"Excuse me, Kyle?" Joe asked towards the back of the store. Kyle practically sprinted to be at Joe's side. "Is there any way we could see one of these in action here in the store? To know if we want to try one of the rentals, I mean."

"Of course," Kyle said. Greg imagined him tacking on, "Anything for you, Jooooe." Kyle walked them to the front of the store, and Greg tried to keep his face turned away from the giant panes of glass. Of course, now the city would actually have pedestrians, casually glancing to see who was shopping in the sexbot store. "We call this one Ralph," Kyle said. "Ralph? Wake up, please," Kyle said in a sing-songy voice. "You can set any activation phrase you'd like. But we do recommend making it something you don't say often. Just to avoid any mishaps when company is over," Kyle said, sharing an oh-so naughty giggle with Joe. The gray strip around its charging port glowed red, then yellow, then green. They stood there for a moment in anticipation. Greg was intrigued, finally able to fight past his embarrassment. He drew closer. He was about to ask if there was something wrong with it.

Ralph turned around swiftly, giving Greg a heart attack. He smiled broadly, but it didn't seem to touch his eyes. "Hello," Ralph said. Joe stuck his hand out and Ralph grabbed it, shaking firmly. "What would you like to do?" Ralph asked.

"Ralph here has a pretty basic AI package. You can ask him to do some rudimentary things. Or even ask him to search the internet for you." Kyle waited for Joe to be impressed, and of course Joe obliged. Greg may as well have been one of the Custom Companions at this point. Furniture you can fuck.

"Ralph," Joe said and Ralph turned his eyes to look at him, "what season of Drummond House are we at?" Ralph's eyes shifted colors a few times before he emitted a soft beep.

"The 14th season of Drummond House recently completed after airing its season finale," Ralph began to say, regurgitating the top search result, Greg guessed. "This count includes offshoots such as Drummond House of Terror and Drummond House All Stars. The recent finale-"

"Thank you, Ralph," Kyle said and Ralph's voice stopped abruptly. His mouth snapped shut and he smiled again.

"What about movement? Does he walk like a robot?" Joe asked. Kyle asked Ralph to step off of the window display and walk to the back of the store. Greg and Joe watched as he did so, walking casually. Naturally, one might say. If not for him strolling into a sea of disembodied limbs and genitals.

"What about, well," Joe said, lowering his voice, "strength calibration. I don't want him breaking my hips or anything."

"Not to worry," Kyle said, "All individual parts and the assembled products are all tested and calibrated. Ralph couldn't hurt a fly."

"Even if I wanted him to?" Joe asked Kyle, but he was staring at Greg to watch his face turn deeper and deeper shades of crimson.

"That's good for now, I think!" Greg said and Kyle remembered he was present. He told them not to hesitate if they had any other questions. When he had walked away, Greg snatched Joe by the arm.

"Get me out of here before you give me a stroke," Greg said sternly. Joe mentioned there was a joke there but Greg gave him a sideways look.

"Thank you!" Kyle called from the back as they opened the door to leave. "Come back and see us sometime!" he said to them, but really to Joe.

The sun had plunged below the horizon by the time they left the store. Greg felt a pang of disappointment. He had wanted to see his final sunset. He didn't say anything to Joe, instead choosing to watch the snowflakes drift across the black sky. It was only after they had been walking for a few minutes did he realize he didn't correct himself when thinking about his "final sunset".

NIGHT

The store Joe took him to was sleepy in every sense of the word, and so was the cashier, an elderly woman, propping her head up on her hand. She barely roused as they entered, giving a short hello and warning them they'd be closing soon due to the snow. "Perfect timing," Joe said, and Greg was a little comforted to see Joe's positive persona active again after their tiff. Maybe hallucinogens and sexbots could solve all kinds of problems. "What are you thinking?" Joe asked, grabbing a basket.

"It's just a few people," Greg said. "Maybe some stuff to make a cheese board? Some plastic plates. I'm sure you noticed, I don't have much in the way of dishes." He thought back to why that was the case. The shattered ceramics he didn't bother cleaning up for a week, the cabinets opened wide like empty caskets. How he only replaced them with the bare minimum.

"Sounds good to me," Joe said. He pointed to a shelf of various wines, stiff paint labels chipping away on green glass. "Red or white? Both?"

"Get whatever you like. I don't drink anymore," Greg said, trying hard not to leave an opening for a question. "I'm not sure what everyone else likes. If they have any decency they'll bring their own," he said and laughed. Joe grabbed a red from the shelf and they kept moving.

"Any particular colors?" Joe asked, gesturing to the selection of plates. Greg grabbed the nearest pack and tossed it into the basket. They found a garland that exclaimed "Happy Birthday!" in bright block letters. Greg hated it, but figured it was as good as anything else. Joe picked up a pack of balloons and Greg got one with fewer to replace it. The less they put up, the less would need to be cleaned the next day.

He had only been to a few 30th parties, and from what he could tell, they ran the gamut. Alissa's had been a fairly wild affair. She rented some rich guy's third house he never used and invited everyone she knew. They all got drunk off their asses and blared music, singing karaoke and dancing til they couldn't stand. This was all well before midnight. Their mother had made the whole day leading up to it worth the drinks. He knew he couldn't understand what she was going through, but her anxiety rolled out like tidal waves, dragging everyone out to sea. Everything had some significance because it might be the last one. But that just made everything feel trite. Finally, Alissa fed her enough wine that she actually had a good time. But Alissa had always been better at defusing their mother, not letting it affect her the way it did Greg.

When the time came, she had everyone stand around her. She was like that, never afraid or ashamed to admit she wanted to be the center of attention. With something like that, she deserved to be. She thanked them all from the bottom of her heart. There wasn't a dry eye in the place. They all held their breath as the clock struck 12 and when she was still there the party ramped up exponentially.

"I love you, little brother," she had said, arm draped over his shoulders, head slumped against his. "I mean it," she said. He told her she was drunk. "Well no shit," she said. She pushed her wild tangle of hair into his face as she dug her cheek into his shoulder and sighed contentedly. "But sober, drunk, dead, or alive, I love you."

He wondered if that was true.

"You alright?" Joe asked. Greg realized he was smiling, thinking back. Four years felt like a lifetime. They were standing in the cheese section and Greg picked a handful at random. "I like this chaotic energy you have right now," Joe said, piling the selections into the basket. Greg did the same with crackers and meat. The meat was all the same thing anyway, just flavored differently.

"Can I ask you something else about being an Ephemera?" Greg asked and Joe nodded. "Is my party going to be sad? Pitiful, I mean? 6 or 7 people standing around my apartment, politely eating cheese, checking their watches for midnight?"

"I don't think I understand the question," Joe said.

"I mean, I assume you've attended far more 30th parties than I have. Right?" Greg asked as they meandered back towards the front. "Just, compared to all of those, is plastic plates and mismatched cheeses...just..."

"Are you worried I'm going to be bored?" Joe asked as he bent down to inspect some noisemakers. They were the crank kind that you whirled around and made an awful racket. He tested one out and Greg asked him to never do it again. "I will say, that in my five years-"

"Five years?" Greg asked, baffled. "So this was your under 30 job too?" It occurred to Greg that Joe must really know how to not be attached. He wasn't a fish slipping into different streams, he was some long-necked bird, lighting on river rocks, ready to leave when he had done what he needed to.

"It was. As I was saying, in my five years as an Ephemera, I have come to find that every person is unique, and so are their parties. Some don't have parties at all." He stopped and laughed to himself for a moment. "One party was actually a chess tournament. The birthday girl destroyed everyone, including me. She wore a crown for the rest of the night."

"Did she..." Greg began and realized what he wanted to ask was rude. But he was a heron, a crane, elegant and detached. Surely he didn't carry every person with him the way average people do.

"She was gone at midnight," Joe said. He said it so matter-of-factly Greg couldn't help but feel it meant the opposite. Maybe some clients left an impression on his heart and others didn't. Which would he be, he wondered. Would Joe be discussing his party a year from now, a week from now, to some lonely heart? Using Greg's party to make them feel better about theirs. Get this, Joe would say, breathing on their ear, this guy had a cheese board. Can you believe it?

They were back in the wine aisle at this point.

"Is that everything?" Joe asked, looking through their haul. Greg pretended to make an inventory, but was really just naming things in the cart. He gave it his approval. For a brief moment, he allowed a positive fantasy to slash through the thick wall of negative daydreams. They were just boyfriends, out doing some shopping before the snow got too bad. Domestic and docile. They had forgotten to make a list, because they always did. Joe selected the cheapest of each item as opposed to the better quality. They would be heading home to make dinner.

The spectre of reality crawled out from behind the wine bottles, then. A cold, dripping finger reaching out to touch the back of Greg's neck. Tracing it down his back, radiating dread through each organ as it went. Never forget.

Tick.

Tock.

They took everything to the cashier, who had already put on her coat. She said she was going to lock up behind them. Costume jewelry dangled from distended earlobes, a bright green beetle brooch pinned to her coat lapels. She smelled of flowers, or whatever it was people put in perfumes to make people think of flowers. Her arthritic fingers punched the touch screen with surprising force so that she had to keep readjusting it back to where she could see it.

Greg wondered what her 30th had been like. Was she working at this age because she wanted to or because she didn't have any kids to take care of her? He spun a complex web of her life, picturing vignettes of good times and bad. "It is your birthday?" she asked and Joe pointed to Greg. She held her hand out and Greg took it. "Good luck to you," she said. "I will be praying."

"That's nice of you," Greg said, "but you don't even know me."

"Why should I have to know you?" she said with a wry smile. Greg conceded that was a fair point. Joe realized they hadn't brought any bags and the cashier gave them some of the store's for free. They thanked her and she waved their thanks out of the air. "Come back and see me sometime," she said.

Back out in the cold, they went towards the nearest subway entrance. "She was fun," Joe said, a bag in each hand.

"Kinda reminds me of my mom," Greg said thoughtfully.

"Because she's an older woman?" Joe asked and chuckled.

"No, I mean her sort of rude kindness," Greg said.

Once they had made it down to the train and got settled in their seats, he checked his phone again. More texts and posts and pictures. He saw another from his mom, this time with a picture attached. It was a picture of him, Alissa, and their mom at the aquarium. Greg was crying, Alissa was smiling maniacally, her back teeth showing and curly hair sticking in every direction. And in the middle was their mom, giving whoever was behind the camera a "you've got to be kidding me" look. Maybe their dad took the picture? He felt as if he remembered this moment, but everything surrounding it was vague and gauzy. "Simpler times," the text read from his mom.

"You were a cute kid," Joe said, looking over at Greg's phone.

"Do you mind?" Greg said, holding it to his chest.

"Oh, come on, show me," Joe said. Greg reluctantly handed it over. "That's you, and I'm guessing that's your mom. Who's that?" his finger hovered over Alissa's face.

"My sister," Greg said. "She's, uh, not here anymore." Greg had the impulse to say "She's dead," but knew that was harsh to most people.

"Didn't make it?" Joe asked casually. "If you don't mind me asking, of course."

"No, she made it," Greg said, examining the picture again. He wondered what he was crying about. "But she was in an accident earlier this year," Greg said.

"Oh," Joe said. "I'm sorry."

"Thanks," Greg said. He tried not to hold it against people who said they were sorry for things like that. He knew it was said with good intentions. And often was the only thing anyone could think to say in response.

"Do you want to talk about it?" Joe asked.

"Uh, well," Greg began, "the long and short of it is that a delivery truck malfunctioned and swerved into the opposite lane. Just right where her car was." An awful momentum took hold of his train of thought. "It was late and no one else was involved. Just a freak accident." Greg cleared his throat. "It was instant, as far as I know." It's all he could think to say.

"That's awful," Joe said quietly.

"Yeah," Greg said, squirming at having this conversation. Addressing the open wound somehow making it worse. Trying to lighten the mood, he said, "She was so excited to plan my party. Even when I said I didn't want a party, she was going to throw one anyway. She knew I wouldn't miss it." Greg thought of her late night texts, when inspiration would come to her. She was strongly in favor of a theme. Costumes and music. He still listened to the playlist from time to time. Just sad gasoline on the sad fire.

"We'll do her proud," Joe said. Greg smiled wanly. "I hope this doesn't come across as making it about me, but just to say I can relate." Joe pulled out his phone and found a particular picture. It was him and what Greg guessed was his twin. They were laughing, arms on each other's shoulders. "My brother didn't make it," Joe said.

The tables had turned on Greg. He desperately needed to not say he was sorry. Greg placed his hand on top of Joe's, instead. "I feel guilty a lot," Greg said, shuffling his feet. "Like it would be better if the roles were reversed."

"I do too," Joe said. He swiped to another picture. His brother in a jersey and grease paint, streaked with sweat. He was shouting, hoisting his helmet about his head. Some epic victory had taken place. "He was the better of the two of us," Joe said, swiping to another picture. Older now, closer to Greg's age. Joe's brother was holding a baby, totally enraptured. "He had more to lose, at the very least."

Greg didn't want to contradict him or tell him how to feel. He had his own things to sort out. But he didn't want that to be the end of the conversation. A real thread began to run between them then, Greg felt. A string strung from his chest to Joe's. There is a certain understanding amongst people that have experienced loss, he had found. Things that no one else can possibly fathom. Things that can't be said by virtue of someone's good fortune of having their entire heart and soul intact. For better or worse, death was a common friend, a foundation that cut through a lot of barriers. Brothers in arms, survivors, comrades. The more they related to one another's tragedy, the string would weave itself into knots and cords. Nevermind the endless strings that radiated off of Joe, some slack and others drawn taut, would give a musical twang if plucked. Greg rested his head on Joe's shoulder and said, "Tell me about him."

Joe tilted his head at the photo, regarding it as if it were a piece in the museum. "He was an idiot, honestly," Joe said, a smile materializing on his face. He was clearly dredging up some happy memories. "But funny. Unbelievably funny. I can't do it justice, but he'd just say things in the goofiest way. Had little rhymes he made up about inane shit." Greg felt a small blip of happiness, knowing this is what he wanted when grief got brought up. He wanted to summon them back through stories and memories. Even if it was just their shade, an opalescent hologram to turn and examine, dust motes drifting in and out of their bodies made of refracted light, it meant they were back. For the briefest moment, Joe's brother was here with them, and so was Alissa. Joe continued, "He could defuse any situation. When we got in trouble, I always hid behind him. He'd make our parents laugh and pretty soon they'd forget why they were so mad in the first place."

"Alissa was like that too," Greg said. "Maybe not as funny, but she thought she was hilarious, and in that way she was." Greg was swept up in the sharing of memories. "Sometimes it was like her and my mom spoke their own language. She could say the exact same thing I did, but our mom would just 'get it' when it came from her." He shrugged his shoulders. "She always said it was because me and my mom are too much alike. I think that very well may be the case."

"I don't want to step out of line by saying this," Joe started, "but I think you should call your mom. I think you'd both feel better." Greg didn't want to hear that, but he knew it was true.

On the journey back up to the surface from the subway tunnels, Greg remembered why he was crying that day at the aquarium. It had been his father's 30th birthday. He couldn't have been older than 5. His parents had tried to explain what might happen to his dad, but that had been a mistake. He spent the entire day, morose, inconsolable. The tank behind them had dolphins in it. They had been the final straw for young Greg's fragile emotional state. He remembered gazing up at them in wonder, the light cascading down into their water in heavenly rays. They seemed to smile as they glided past the glass. The only word he had for it was "magical". For the first time that day, he had forgotten what had made him so sad. But Alissa had sidled up next to him and in a child's whisper, that is to say a breathy shout, told him the dolphins weren't real. They were robots. Dolphins were almost all dead, she said, as if she were telling a ghost story. Their mom scolded Alissa, but she had inflicted the wound she meant to. There was no unlearning it. He turned to his mother, betrayed, and she told him the truth. Most of the animals they saw that day were animatronics. But that just meant the real animals were out in the wild, living happy lives.

This did nothing to alleviate his disappointment.

Greg had next to no memories from that time in his life now, but he had an image of his dad, bleared by tears. A striped shirt, most of his face obscured by his phone as he held it out to take a picture.

Greg knew what he looked like, thanks to pictures, but couldn't form it in his mind. He had no idea what he sounded like, what hobbies he had. He disappeared and the world kept spinning. His things gradually disappeared from the house as well. By the time Greg was leaving to live on his own, what few remnants remained of his father had been relegated to a storage tote. Tucked away in a closet somewhere, mouldering relics too important to toss but too painful to live in the light.

It filled Greg with a peculiar kind of dread to think that he was now as old as his dad would ever be. By his age, his father had been married and had two children. He had owned his own business. His father had seen how rare real paper was becoming and wanted to help save printed books. Having a sizable library of his own, his father used that as his initial stock. He would take trips, rounding up any book he could find. Someone would eventually buy it was his reasoning.

After that, he had worked with local creators to print new books on pretty much anything else you could think of. The store carried displays meant primarily for use as ereaders and did some basic maintenance on them as well. The true glory, people told Greg, was that it *felt* like a bookstore. They curated a quiet environment, played mellow music. Had cushy chairs for readers and hopeful novelists to sit and work. He didn't remember a time without the bookstore, so it was just another place to be bored for a lot of his life. Most of the shelves just had dummy books on them, boxes painted to look like spines. He had been snotty about that in his teen years. How terribly *phony* it all was.

From what Greg gathered from the nostalgic tales told around Thanksgiving tables, his father had been driven, stubborn. Maybe a bit prideful, but he had a lot to have pride in. Although Greg had never uttered it aloud to anyone else, he resented his father for it. He knew there was nothing that he could have done differently. He just lived his life until he didn't anymore. But a clot of anger had formed in his heart and only grew larger as he got older, and started to understand what it meant to not have him.

When they stepped out of the subway entrance and started walking home, Greg called his mom. The phone barely rang before she picked it up. "Greg?" she asked. She had been crying. Her voice was hoarse, her nose congested.

"Hey, mom," he said. "You okay?"

"Oh honey," she said, her voice warbly. "I just kept thinking if I didn't- what if I never got to talk to you again? This would be the only birthday you've ever had that I didn't get to hear your voice." She took a deep breath, trying to pull up on the emotional nosedive. "I just really didn't like how we left off yesterday."

"It's okay," Greg said. "I didn't either. I'm sorry."

The day before, he had gone to see her at the bookstore. Neutral ground, he thought. It was already so laden with memories, what was one more? He had stood outside the door for a while, huffing his ecig and shivering in the bright daylight. Greg was rehearsing what he'd say. He came to tell her goodbye, make a point to say goodbye and to hug and cry or whatever she wanted. Somewhere in there he'd mention how he would rather her not be at the party. Simple.

Eventually she had caught sight of him out of the store windows. The bell above the door chimed and it startled him. "Quit puffing that thing and get in here before your fingers fall off," she said. He complied, entering the bookstore. He kept his eyes low, the bearer of bad news. A few customers sat in the lounge area, working diligently or taking a nap. He noticed his mom had put in a fake fireplace on the far wall. Above it hung an enormous oil painting in the style of an Edwardian portrait. His dad stood tall in a nice suit, Alissa sat in an armchair beside him wearing a pale blue dress. He didn't think his dad had even owned a suit. And Alissa seemed gaunt, her skin tone all wrong.

"Oh, I had that commissioned," his mom said, catching Greg looking. "I gave the guy a couple pictures of 'em and he came up with that. Isn't that wild?" He agreed that it was, indeed, wild. "You'd have seen it a few months ago if you ever came around," she said, moving to the back area where the office was. He didn't like the stage that he was walking onto.

The carpet in the room was enough to evoke a torrent of memories. He used to hide away in the office when his mom was busy with the shop. When he needed to not be underfoot. He had spent countless hours staring up at the ceiling, waging intergalactic war and unearthing hidden ruins in his mind. He wondered what had happened to all those figments. Could he dredge them back up if he tried hard enough? Or had his imagination been amputated?

She offered him the chair, but he told her to sit. When she did he realized how small she was. Had she shrunk? Maybe that heavy grief didn't just feel like a black hole. Maybe by the time he was her age he'd be the size of a cicada.

"Are you all set for your party?" she asked. "I think I'll bring a cake. I know red velvet is your favorite." He tried to smile at this, but couldn't make it seem genuine because it didn't feel genuine.

"About the party, mom," he began, unable to look her in the eye.

"You're not picking some crazy venue last minute, right? You know your sister's party about killed me," she said.

"Well, I think we both know what happened at Alissa's party," Greg said, leaning against the wall.

"What's that mean?" his mom asked. Her arms went crossed. Shit, he was fucking it up. This was supposed to be a soft blow. An easy let down. He was going to make it out like he was doing her a favor.

"I don't want you to take this the wrong way," he said, knowing there was only one way to take it. It was bad. He was being heartless. "But I don't want you at the party tomorrow." Her face dropped. She asked if he was serious. "Yes, I am," he said, also crossing his arms. "You can't come." She threw her hands in the air. "I want to be able to have fun with my friends." And his hired Ephemera, he thought to himself. "I'm going to be a nervous wreck as it is and you'll just make it worse."

"So I don't get to be at my only baby's party?" she said. She was gutted. But also incredibly furious. "I'll make you think 'you can't come'! I know where you live. I'll be there!"

"Mom, I'm serious," Greg said. "Don't come." He rubbed his face in agitation. "We did dinner the other day, remember? We looked at a bunch of old pictures and got really sad. Remember? I thought that was pretty clearly your send off for me."

"Forgive me for being a little sad, sometimes," his mom said, her voice raising slightly. "I happen to have a lot to be sad about."

"No shit, mom," he said, matching her tone and going a little louder. "Everyone's got shit to be sad about." He thought of the painting above the fireplace, his dad and sister gazing out at him forlornly. As if to say, "You're next." Their weird imitation mouths twitching to say, "Just wait."

Her lips went thin and her eyes were ablaze. But she shrugged. "Well, if that's all you have to say," she said. It wasn't all he had to say. Not by a long shot. But she turned away from him, idly clicking around on her desk display. The conversation was over. The ball was in her court, but she had taken the net down.

"Alright," he said and stepped out of the office, "bye."

The patrons in the store were all looking at one another, exchanging quiet murmurs. His face flushed with red shame as he ran for the door. He turned back to see the painting again. He wanted to burn it. Take a knife and slit it into scraps. He wasn't sure how he would manage to do both at the same time, but it felt like the only thing that might bring him some shred of happiness.

He had ducked into an alley to wait out the resulting panic attack. In heaving gasps he took in the frigid air. It burned his nose and lungs. Why was he such a piece of shit, he wondered to himself. The entire thing had just been so *him*. And it had been so her as well. Equal part martyr and victim, doused with emotion and pettiness. All his best traits, really.

The thought that made him feel the worst slithered up from the depths of his mind, which was weakened by his panicked state. He wondered to himself, out of all the combinations of who stayed and who went, why were they the last two left? There had to be some God or higher power out there because it was a sick joke. The moment he felt the thought, he hung his head.

He wished a lightning bolt would just strike him dead.

Make it quick. Stop making me wait.

"I'm sorry too," she said. They were silent for a moment, Greg unlocking the door to his apartment building. "Well what are you doing? You're not alone are you?" she asked.

"I'm with a friend," he said.

"Like...a *friend*?" she asked.

"Mom," he said.

"Okay, sorry. Did you ever look into that thing? Eefema? Affirma?" she asked. Joe couldn't catch his laughter in time.

"Oh my God, can he hear me?" she asked, scandalized.

"Half the city can hear you. You scream on the phone," he said. They were walking through the lobby. He checked the mail out of habit and found Peter's present. He had totally forgotten. His mother said something but he was lost for a second. "I'm sorry, what?"

"Are you sure he's, uh, he's safe, you know?" she asked, but much louder this time. Joe gave him a bemused look of bewilderment. "I just worry about you younger generation. We didn't have all that when I turned 30."

"Not that it's any of your business," Greg said, "but yes. Ephemera's have to get regular health check-ups." What he didn't say was he obsessively researched the topic. Had gone onto message boards and seen the evidence of their policy, of it being enforced. Joe gave him an impressed look. They hadn't touched on that in any of their conversation.

"Which you need to do too," his mom countered. "I just wish…" she began and Greg felt his shoulders draw up in defense. She was struggling with the words, so he told her to spit it out as kindly as he could. "I hope that after all this maybe you can find happiness. Find someone nice. Get me some grandbabies." Greg could only let out a frustrated groan. "Alissa didn't get the chance, and I just hate that." He knew he and his mother were cut from the same cloth. That she wasn't trying to pluck his nerves, but for her own sanity, she had to get the words out of her body. "You could've been building that life this whole time, is all."

"And what?" Greg asked, his shout bouncing off the walls in the lobby. A maintenance robot whirred past, swiveling its round head up at him and Joe. Greg flipped it the bird. Joe stood there, helplessly. "You know they won't let under 30s adopt. So you're saying you hoped I had knocked someone up?" Joe set the bags down and gave him a gesture of "I'll give you some space." The lobby filled with a gust of cold air as Joe stepped outside. "How irresponsible is that?" Greg had grown tired of figuring out the right way to say things. "What if I do die tonight? I'd just leave my partner to fend for themselves?" He let out a grunt of consternation. "Like dad? Who left you alone with two kids and a bookstore to figure out?" He had wanted to say "fuck up" but he didn't truly feel that or think it was true. Just words that bumped against the angry red insides of his brain. "Are you seriously going to tell me that's what you envisioned for yourself?"

"That's not what I'm saying at all," she said, getting defensive as well. "You may think we were reckless, but we waited until after my 30th to even think about having kids." They both let the fuzzy silence settle for a moment. "I wouldn't do a single thing differently." She cleared the crying phlegm from her throat. He breathed deeply and cleared his throat as well to let her know he was still on the line. "I'll admit," she said, "I can't handle you not being here. I'll be the last one left. And that's a horrible feeling."

"I can't imagine," he said, his head leaned against the wall, "but I know you're scared." He built a little resolve. This may indeed be the last time he got to talk to her. If he was to have any closure, it would have to be sealed at this moment. "I just need you to understand," he said and took a deep breath, "that your idea of happiness is not what I want for myself. If I make it, I'm not sure what I'm going to do. But I don't think kids are part of it." She gave an acquiescing hmmm. "I could move or start a new job and I might still be unhappy. I really don't need any extra pressure." He leaned back against the cold tile wall and closed his eyes. "Wherever I go, there I'll be."

"Oh, honey. I know. Whatever it means for you to be happy, that's what I want for you, okay?" The edge had left her voice. She sounded utterly defeated, and that tore Greg's heart into sinewy bits.

"Well," Greg said plainly, "as much as I love being lectured, I have to get set up for the party." The line was quiet. "I'm kidding, mom. I love you."

"So still no invite to the party, huh?" she asked.

"I can't have you competing for Joe's attention," he said and she laughed. She asked about him and he gave her some highlights. "I gotta go, mom. The elevator's going to cut us off. I'll talk to you tomorrow, okay?"

"Okay. Tomorrow. Talk to you then." Greg thought that was all she had to say, but as he pulled the phone from his ear, her voice echoed out into the lobby. "And if not, I'll see you again. Whenever that may be," she said with conviction. When she got called to heaven she meant. "Me, you, and Alissa. Your dad, too. Just like old times."

"Of course," he said, wishing he could believe it too.

"I love you," she said. They traded "I love you"s a few hundred more times.

He was finally the first one to hang up and he let out a pent up sigh of relief.

Greg peeled himself off the wall and went to find Joe outside, leaving the bags on the floor. Joe heard the door opening behind him, stood from his squatting position, and turned. His face was flush from the cold wind, snowflakes caught in his hair. A snow plow robot stood at his feet, bumping into his shoes.

"I keep trying to set it back on the sidewalk but it keeps coming back to me," Joe said. He stepped out of its way and it froze, thinking for a second before adjusting its trajectory and aiming for his feet again. Joe was tickled by the situation and it was just what Greg needed to lighten his spirits, even slightly. "Can we keep him?" Joe asked, picking it up. It waved its plow up and down, whirring loudly.

"It'll make a mess," Greg said, leaning against the rail. "Not to mention, we've already got a kid and they're a handful." The phone call with his mom was still raw in his mind. A bruise he kept touching. But the bruise was better than not taking the plunge, he supposed.

Joe walked a few feet down the sidewalk and set the robot down. It thought for a moment more and then continued on its correct path, scattering salt behind it. Joe watched it go, clearly proud of himself for figuring it out. He looked up at Greg as the Christmas lights began to switch on. His face flashed from red to blue to green, and Greg liked all of them. "Feel better?" Joe asked.

"Not if you get to say 'I told you so'," Greg said and raked a bit of snow from the railing in Joe's direction. Joe asked if he was ready to head up. Greg held the door open for him.

"Are you gonna open your present?" Joe asked, nodding towards the little package in Greg's hand.

"Oh. Yeah, but I'll wait until we get inside." Greg realized he was still holding the box, had slightly crushed it in his fist while on the phone with his mom. They went back through the lobby, collecting their party supplies, and rode the elevator up to Greg's floor. They got everything through the door and onto the counter. "I'll be right back," he said, going into his bedroom and closing the door. He pulled the lid of the box open.

He found a silver coin and a note inside. It read: "A good luck charm. My dad gave it to me before my party. You can give it back to me on Monday." Greg took the coin from the box and turned it over. It was just a quarter, dull and slightly discolored. But he drug his thumb along the bumps around its edge and along Washington's face. It was probably one of the last of its kind, escaping the government buyback of physical money, however many years ago. He felt the heft of it transferring it from palm to palm until it was warm from his touch. He thought about Peter at his party, before they became friends. Cool, collected Peter nervously flipping the coin between his fingers in his pocket. Greg saw that the minted year was quite old, and wondered how many other people it had met, brushed against, been traded between to and fro. This little slab of metal that had likely been buried between couch cushions or had sat neglected in a car's cup holder lucked out, had avoided the fate of its kin. Was now a holy relic, a good luck charm that warded off danger and signified survival. He laughed at himself, doubting there was that much symbolism in it, but appreciated it all the same.

He placed the quarter on his desk and savored the clack it made. He pulled out his phone and texted Peter to tell him thank you. Peter's reply came, telling Greg not to worry about it. A second text came, an addendum, ripping off a bandage, to say that Peter wasn't coming to the party. He said he felt awful about it. Greg felt a pang of disappointment, but he understood. Things happen. Sometimes people aren't comfortable being around someone who might be dying. Dropping his gift off should have been a sign, but Greg directed his thoughts to being grateful.

He decided to check the other messages he had dismissed throughout the day. Hidden amongst the Happy Birthdays and well wishes were expressions of condolences over the party. Something had come up. They had come down with a bug. There was some crisis at their job. Greg's face grew hot as he went down the list.

No one he had invited was going to come.

A hot wave of shame rushed up from his gut. It set his teeth on edge.

He tore out of his bedroom to find Joe trying to pin the banner up by himself. "Don't bother," Greg said and dug through the bags to find one of the cellophane sealed cheeses. He tore off its wrapper and took a bite out of it. Pungent and sour, but he had made it this far.

"What's the matter?" Joe asked, dropping the big block letters to the ground. "What happened?"

Chewing past the cheese, Greg showed him his phone. He selected the messages that said they weren't coming. There weren't that many to begin with, but absolutely no one could make it, Greg explained. Joe scrolled through the messages, his face lit up once more in the ambient white glow. "At the very least we could've not bought all this stupid shit." Greg picked up some of the plastic plates and tossed them back down in disgust.

Joe came to stand beside him and rested his head against Greg's. "I'm sorry," he said quietly. "I know it hurts."

"What do you know about it?" Greg asked, mumbling. He felt Joe tense slightly before he brought his arms around Greg like a vice grip. Greg felt contained, confined.

"You asked about other people's parties before," Joe said. "You may think I'm bullshitting you when I say this," he said, letting go of Greg and picking up his phone. He held it in front of Greg and scrolled through the messages, having to go through several pages. "Not one of my clients has ever received this many well wishes and good lucks." He set the phone back down on the counter. "Your friends may not be able to be here, but they are thinking of you." Greg absorbed this, wanting it to mean something, but the bubbling from below carried Joe's words away. "You could always call your mom. I'm sure she'd be happy to come."

"I'm going for a cigarette," Greg said, finding his coat. He yanked open the balcony's sliding door and pulled it shut again. The outside world was cold and beautiful. Snow still fell, listless, dancing on drafts of wind. Which snowflakes got to be with the others and get made into snowmen and snowballs? And which ones landed on a warm streetlamp or errant tongue and dissolved in an instant? His fingers already growing numb from the cold, he fished a cigarette out of the pack and lit it. He still had so many left. He could just sit out here and smoke them all. Let the cold take him. His steam breath mixed with the smoke and drifted up and away in the night sky.

No one else was out on their balconies. Even the streets were empty of cars. He could very well convince himself he was the last person left alive. Which fate would be worse, he wondered. Leaving everyone or being left. What if there was nothing good for him on the other side of midnight? He'd have to go back to work, if not at the office, then somewhere. Bills would still have to be paid. Meals made. Days measured in pills that can only treat symptoms, never cure the cause. Because he was the cause.

Decades and decades of subsisting.

Struggling up the stream.

Surviving didn't mean living.

He realized he was peering off the railing of the balcony now to the sidewalk below. If he didn't make it, in the many different meanings of the phrase, no one would know. His body, every trace of him would be gone at midnight. He'd be another snowflake, landing on the sidewalk.

The door slid open behind him and he turned away from the rail. Joe didn't have a coat on, but stood unfazed by the cold wind.

"Any better?" he asked. Greg shook his head, feeling guilt at admitting it.

"I know I should feel grateful," Greg said, slightly punching the railing. "I know people care," he said, having to look away from Joe's eyes. "But...shit. It sucks."

"Don't worry about shoulds," Joe said softly. "I didn't mean to make you feel worse. It does suck. You can feel bad and grateful at the same time." Greg nodded at this, taking a draw off the cigarette. "I didn't have a party, you know," Joe said. "On purpose. My parents threw one for me and my brother, but I let him have the limelight." He breathed in the night and exhaled clouds. "I didn't want any of my friends to know.. I actually took an Ephemera gig on my birthday." Greg raised an eyebrow. "I was weird about it. I didn't want to make a fuss."

"But what if you had disappeared in the middle of the gig?" Greg asked, his mind wandering away from his own trouble.

"That was part of the thrill, if I'm being honest," Joe said, a devilish smirk on his face. "I made sure me and my client had sex at midnight of my birthday. I would be distracted when the moment came, and if I didn't make it...well, they'd have one hell of a story."

"You're sick," Greg said, laughing, "A deviant. Who are you, anyway?" He hoped it conveyed the lack of malice he felt. "When you're not Joe the Ephemera, I mean."

"Maybe you'll find out," Joe said with a smirk and stepped back in. "Come inside when you're ready, okay?" His voice was gentle. Talking down a temper tantrum. But Greg would take the pity tonight.

He could afford to indulge. Joe slid the door shut again and disappeared into the dark apartment.

When Greg had caught his breath again, he peered in through the door. Joe was still preparing the cheese plate, cutting around the chunk Greg had bitten out of the one piece. He watched as Joe brought the plate to the coffee table, then went back and poured two glasses of wine. Greg finished the cigarette and went back inside. "We never finished the episode earlier," Joe said. He had turned the T.V. back on to Drummond House where they had left off. "It'll take your mind off things."

"You're right," Greg said, peeling off his coat. He sat on the couch and piled some cheese on a cracker. He chewed it, staring at the glass of wine Joe sat in front of him. He had forgotten what wine tasted like, but he could smell it from where he sat. It soured his stomach. "I don't drink," he said.

"Oh, shit. I'm sorry. You told me that." Joe picked it up and poured it into his own glass. "There. Can I get you some water or something?" Greg didn't answer but Joe got up and came back with a glass of water. "Do you want to talk about it? Or anything?"

"Maybe after the show," Greg said. They ate the cheese and meat-flavored protein slices. As the episode went on, they eventually gravitated to Greg leaning against Joe, who placed an arm around him. Greg would give him the backstory on why one contestant hated another. Joe would eat a cracker, then feed one to Greg, then repeat the process. By the end of the hour and a half special the cheese board was ravaged, a few crumbs serving as the only wreckage left behind.

"Wow," Joe said as the credits played. "They really did a lot of bitching."

"Right? I love how stupid it is," Greg said. "I'm glad I got to watch the season finale. That would have been a major point of unfinished business."

"Do you have many of those?" Joe asked, his face in Greg's hair.

"No, not really. I mean, lots of people accomplished astounding things before 30. And I, well...I didn't. But I don't think I really aspired to much. It didn't matter to me to see the Eiffel Tower or run a cross country marathon. That all seemed like busywork, honestly." They sat in silence for a moment, washed in the glow of the television. "There are tons of films I still want to watch, but I know that's a fool's errand. I could've watched movies 24/7 and still never seen them all." Joe hmmed in agreement. "Y'know, if I'm being honest, though, I do wish I had made more time to make films."

"Oh!" Joe said, leaning up and taking his arm away. "Why don't you show me your films?" He was so genuinely excited, eyes bright.

"I don't know about that," Greg said, already feeling embarrassed.

"Please? I'll answer any of your Ephemera questions if you do. Even if I don't want to." Joe made pleading hands paired with exaggerated pouty lips. Greg gave in, secretly a little pleased that someone would see them before he died. If he died. Greg accessed the files on his phone and cast them to the T.V.

"This first one was-" Greg began.

"Shh!" Joe said earnestly. "Don't spoil anything. I want to see them uninformed."

There were three in total, one for each year he was in the film program. The first was landscape shots he filmed throughout the year, voiced over by recordings of Sylvia Plath reading her own poems. They were important ones to him, but he remembered how his classmates called him pretentious. And maybe he was. But even then, fresh from high school, he was worried about this exact point in his life. Plath had been 30 when she died. She had made it. But she couldn't keep on living.

If he made it, would he have a similarly inescapable end? The medication meant to help Sylvia only made things worse. Greg understood that all too well. Four words comprised the note Plath left behind. For a while, Greg had been obsessed with figuring out what his four words might be, but assumed they might be similar. He had started saving money, the taped seal around the door leading to his mother and sister.

Joe had never heard of Plath, so Greg gave him a brief biography, the details as slightly fuzzy as the bees her father kept. Joe asked for the next one, and Greg complied.

The second was an attempt at horror. Greg had been invited to a party, which wasn't common, and he asked if he could film the people there. They all agreed, thinking it would be interviews. Instead, he waited until the night had drawn out and people had kind of forgotten he was there. He filmed from outside the windows. People talking, laughing. A brief glimpse of a kiss as he continued to walk past. Smash cuts of intense close-ups of eyes and mouths, discomforting in the near silence. He hoped to capture literally and figuratively being on the outside. How you could only see, but not experience any of the other senses while being that removed. In review, his classmates had told him it was weird, but not necessarily scary. He accepted that.

Joe didn't have much to say on this one. He echoed the sentiment that it was weird and off-putting. But in an interesting way, he made sure to point out. What a saint he was, enduring this schlock.

Greg moved on to the final piece, his stomach already in knots.

His final project had been a music video. He had selected a song from a genre that Zeke teasingly called "Sad Girl". It was a sad song, Greg had to concede. Lots of pining and mourning how people grow apart. For the video, he had filmed Zeke at random moments for candid footage. Chopping up an onion, talking on the phone with his mom. He had included some close-ups of things he loved the most about Zeke. His hands, his eyes, the dimple in his chin. Greg hadn't watched this since he had presented it in class. He knew it was there for those moments he missed Zeke so bad it caused his stomach to cramp. But he had refused. Some stupid notion of the dignity of refusing medication. He was crying now, desperately wanting to bury his face in his hands, but not wanting to look away. It ended with Greg walking behind Zeke in the park, until he realized Greg was recording. Zeke laughed and tried to cover his face. He took off his scarf and pressed it to the camera lens, providing a fade to black as the last note of the song drifted into silence.

"I see," Joe said. "That was beautiful. Clearly made with your heart."

"Thanks," Greg said, wiping his cheeks with his shirt. "He was a good subject."

"Can I ask what happened?" Joe asked.

Greg sat searching for the right way to say it. He had so rarely spoken of it, he didn't have the rote memorization, no muscle memory of euphemisms and informative doublespeak. "I guess the easiest way to put it is he didn't make it." He took a deep breath, trying to stem the flow of words. There was so much to say, he figured chronologically would make more sense. "We started dating in my last year at school. Met on a dating app, of course. Sub30, of all things." Greg chuckled ruefully. It was one of those that you selected yes or no on, more or less just based on a picture. There was a stopwatch in the corner. 30 seconds, how clever, to decide if you found this person attractive or not.

"I was crazy about him immediately." He thought back to their first date. Could so vividly picture Zeke throwing his head back and laughing from his gut. Greg couldn't remember from what, but he liked to imagine it was some witty joke no one else would have understood. "But he required some warming up." The next time they saw each other came to mind, when Greg, his heart perpetually on his sleeve, had to profess his feelings. Zeke recoiled from this. Didn't want to get too attached. They both still had to endure their respective 30ths, after all. But they kept seeing each other, kept talking. Late night texts, watching old movies. "We took things slow. Then we moved in here together after a couple of years."

Greg looked at the kitchen, could swear he saw an imprint of Zeke against the fridge. The last few words he ever got to say. Joe squeezed Greg's leg. No longer "are you nervous?", but "are you okay?" Greg felt he was in the confessional. Forgive me, Joe, for I have sinned against myself and others. "He had his party here. We couldn't really afford more than that. I- I got fucked up on wine and liquor. I was just so nervous. And scared. God, I was scared." He began to cry again. "And he tried. He tried telling me to slow down. He wanted me to remember, just in case." He finally planted his palms against his eyes, speaking into his legs. "He put me to bed before midnight." A shuddering breath. "And then- and then everyone was gone. Everyone."

Joe placed his hand on Greg's back and rubbed it in broad sweeps. "It's okay," he said.

"How is it okay?" Greg's eyes felt like sandpaper as he rubbed at them. "I fucked up. I fucked up so bad and there's nothing I can do to fix it." Greg sobbed, his mournful tears turning to panicked heaves. Joe handed him the glass of water on the table and told him to drink. Greg started to refuse, but Joe opened Greg's hand and placed the glass in his hand.

"Focus on what you can feel, what you can see," Joe said. "The glass is cool. The water is clear. I'm here beside you." Greg took a gulp of the water and nearly choked. But the shock of it started to shake him out of his downward spiral.

"You're good at this," Greg said, trying to be funny.

"We take crisis management courses," Joe said with no malice but it still stung slightly. "I think they've helped me more than I've been able to help people, honestly."

"Crisis managed," Greg said, finishing the water. "I'm not going to jump off the balcony or anything. Promise."

"Do you want to talk about it anymore?" Joe asked.

"No," he felt Zeke standing outside the balcony glass. In the bedroom doorway. Talking about him made him more real. Brought him back like the others, but he carried a big blade buried in his back that Greg didn't want to look at.

"Would you like to ask me anything else about being an Ephemera? I promised, after all," Joe said. "Or anything else about me. I'll tell you the truth." He pulled Greg onto his chest and leaned back.

"What time is it?" Greg asked, a sudden jolt of anxiety coursing through him.

"We still have plenty of time," Joe said, rubbing his back. Greg tried to put it all out of his mind. Do what Joe had said. Focus on what he could feel. The softness of Joe's shirt. And the body within it. The slow rise and fall of Joe's chest as he breathed.

"Okay," Greg took a deep breath and sunk into Joe a little more. "What's your real name?"

"Paul," Joe said without hesitation.

"I like Joe better," Greg said and they laughed together.

Greg asked the sort of things you might ask on a first date. He was from the next state over. He grew up in the country. He didn't prefer dogs or cats over one another, but he had a dog, which was a hassle with clients sometimes. His friend was dog sitting for him as they spoke. He was not in a relationship at the moment, but he was always straightforward with potential partners. That was Joe, Greg thought to himself. Honest, straight-forward Joe. Nevermind his name was Paul. Nevermind he was getting paid to be here.

"Have you ever cancelled a client?" Greg asked, testing the water.

"Yes. Several, actually." Joe cleared his throat. "I told you before that people can get a little crazy on their last day. One nearly got me arrested. I cancelled the contract immediately and got the hell out of there."

"So, uh," Greg said, feeling a fluttering in his stomach he hadn't in untold centuries. "You haven't cancelled on me yet. So you're here because you want to be?" A nervous gurgle ran through him.

"Yes," Joe said. "You're a good person." He squeezed Greg slightly. "If it tells you anything, I've never given my real name to a single client. Or told any of them about my brother." That did make Greg feel good. Important. Worthy. "I always use names I get off a random name generator and try not to repeat them if I can help it. Or I steal one from whatever show I'm watching at the time. I spent an entire summer as a 'Chad' and thought about using it long term." Joe began drawing circles on Greg's back with a single finger. It sent a shiver up and down his spine and he felt his heart quickening.

"Okay, this might be awkward, but I need to ask." Greg pressed his face into Joe's chest, not wanting to look anywhere near his face when he asked. "Have you ever fallen in love with a client?" Greg nearly blurted, his heart pounding. An excruciating few seconds of silence passed. But Joe's finger never stopped drawing endless loops within loops, a mandala of tingles forming in their wake.

"I fall a little bit in love with all of them," Joe said.

"That sounds like a line," Greg said, turning his head so his chin rested on Joe's sternum.

"I told you I'd tell you the truth. That's the truth of it." He wasn't looking at Greg, but his face was deadly serious. "I have dedicated my life to making people happy. And I think that's certainly a kind of love." Joe's hand stopped its rhythmic rubbing. "I remember all of them. And whatever happens to you tonight," his eyes found Greg's and they stared at one another for an unbreathing moment. "I will remember you too." He brought his hand to Greg's cheek and stroked it with his thumb. He was not a fish sliding in amongst the others, or a bird of prey plucking them from the stream. He was the rock in the river bed, smooth and round, capable of being many things to many different creatures. A hiding place, or a tool. Greg could smell the faintest bit of wine coming off of Joe's breath, which was starting to get faster. Coming from him, it didn't evoke the same disgust. Greg wanted to taste it for himself. "You can say no, of course," Joe asked, suddenly quiet. "But would you like to go to bed?"

The darkness of Greg's bedroom was illuminated by the orange ember glow of a cigarette. Sweat clung to his skin and he didn't bother wiping it off. Joe came back into the room, carrying a glass of water.

He took a long gulp of it, standing in the light of the doorway, stark naked. He looked at Greg as he drank the water as if to say, "you like what you see?" Show off, Greg thought. Joe handed him the water and he took a drink. "How do you feel?" Joe asked, sitting on the edge of the bed, where he had that morning. Greg thought about the time that had inched by since that moment. Forever and the blink of an eye.

"I feel great," Greg said. He was tired. It had been too long. But it was a good tired. And this cigarette was icing on the cake. Maybe it was Joe's expertise, but Greg knew he didn't imagine the fun they were having. And it was supposed to be fun, wasn't it?

Greg was a little disappointed in himself for just now figuring it out. The moments before his life might end forever. The other hook-ups and one night stands were attractive, but he didn't even bother trying to connect with them. He had just wanted the mechanical, animal urge to feel good from sex. Be like so many others and be able to still be guarded while being completely naked. But it seemed he wasn't made that way.

"It looks like you're about to go to sleep," Joe said, laying down and draping an arm over Greg. Their skin stuck together in a way that grossed Greg out, but he thought, these were the sensations to savor. He'd probably miss them terribly when he was a ghost or reincarnated as a starfish or whatever was going to happen.

"No time for that," Greg said, taking a draw from the cigarette. "Y'know, I feel bad," he said, examining the paper the tobacco was rolled in as the flame gradually ate at its edes. "Paper is this precious thing and here I am burning it."

"It was already made into a cigarette," Joe said, himself sounding a little sleepy. "It was born to burn, I guess."

"I don't like where this is headed," Greg said, trying to laugh. He finished the cigarette and tossed it into the water glass. "Not much time left," Greg said, running a hand through Joe's hair. "Think we should get ready?"

"It's up to you," Joe said quietly. "We can sleep through it all if you want." His eyes were shut, a hand on Greg's belly as if it were a pillow.

"That sounds nice," Greg said and took a deep breath. He began to say something else but realized Joe had drifted off, snoring softly into his ribs. In the quiet warmth of the moment, Greg allowed himself to daydream. Just for a moment, he thought. Just for right now. Joe had surprised Greg for his birthday, after acting like he had had nothing planned. Had let Greg stew in his frustration. After a long day, a great day, they were finally crashing. Greg looked down at Joe's placid face and was free to smile. What a beautiful little life they had together. An ice crystal suspended in the air, refracting light and gleaming like a distant, cold star. In the 11th hour, reality held no sway, could do nothing to shatter the reflections of them stretching on through time. Laughing until they couldn't breath, aggravated arguments, legs in laps and hurried kisses goodbye. Going to parties, getting drunk, begrudgingly taking care of the other when they spent the rest of the night hugging the toilet. Taking trips. Growing old. Trying to make sense of the world as it continued to move, ever onward. Funerals, weddings, another 50 some odd years of birthdays.

All these fragments slipped through Greg's mind in the moment it took Joe to wake up again and laugh softly, embarrassed he had fallen asleep. Greg kissed Joe on top of his head before he said, "I want to go through the whole rigamarole. Just in case."

"You didn't strike me as the superstitious type," Joe said, stretching and making to move off the bed, unaware of the entire life he had lived with Greg while he was dreaming. Generally, Greg wasn't prone to believing in luck. If such a thing existed, he had only ever had the bad kind. But maybe that was Karma. A lifetime of big and little tragedies to put some meaning into making it. He eventually got up as well and the two went to the bathroom. They showered and Joe washed Greg's hair, scrubbed his body. This was meant to make the body clean, literally of course, but also to rinse away the past 30 years. It felt more like a body being prepared for embalming. By the end he was getting frustrated with how small the shower was, how Joe kept bumping him into the knobs on the wall. But at the end, as Joe was rinsing off the suds, Greg saw his lips barely moving, unable to hear what he was muttering. He decided to leave it be, in case it was a superstition of his own, the one thing that might end up saving him.

After they had dried off, Joe helped Greg get dressed. Greg pulled his funeral suit from the closet and laid it out on the bed. It still smelled of funeral parlor flowers and graveyard dirt. He had worn it to Zeke's funeral and Alissa's. He had gotten the bang for his buck, he guessed. He stepped into the pants as Joe held them, and lifted them up to his waist. He buttoned them, wrapping his arms around Greg and kissing him softly on the neck. Next came the shirt, the tie, the coat. Another gesture of anointment that just made him feel like he was already dead.

Next came the good luck charms. Greg went to the bathroom and applied Avni's red lipstick with a fumbling hand. It had a peculiar smell he hadn't noticed before. He turned to Joe and gave a Marilyn Monroe pout. "It's your shade," Joe said, leaning on the doorframe. Greg wasn't sure, but he thought Joe seemed genuinely sad. "I might make it you know," Greg said, eyeing him as he blotted the lipstick, assuming he was doing it right.

"You very well might," Joe said and shifted his weight off the door frame.

"It's a shame we'll never see each other after this," Greg said, sidling past Joe and returning to his room.

"Stranger things have happened," Joe said. He still hadn't gotten dressed. Was he sulking? "Besides, maybe we'll both end up as fish in the same stream a hundred years from now." Greg smiled at this.

"I'll likely just be a rock on the river bed," Greg said.

"A bit of moss on a tree, maybe?" Joe said. He left to get dressed.

Greg picked up Peter's quarter from his desk and held it at his heart for a moment. He placed it in his right pocket. He placed the lipstick tube in the left. He checked his phone one last time. He was surprised to see even more messages. This time, he took time to appreciate them. Avni sent him a picture of her and Trish. They were drunk and very happy. Some people he hadn't talked to in years had come out of the woodwork. Maybe after all this he would make a point to catch up with them. He turned his phone off and placed it beside his display. For a brief moment, he considered scrubbing his browsing history, but he was beginning to see it Joe's way. If he didn't make it, what did it matter for whoever came after him to know what kind of porn he watched?

He left his bedroom and examined himself in the bathroom mirror, straightening his tie. He slicked his hair to the side. He felt dolled up. A body in the coffin or a body in the pew, he certainly felt ready for a funeral.

When he went into the living room, he found Joe dressed in some slacks and a dress shirt, unbuttoned to his chest, the sleeves rolled up. He had found an internet live stream on the T.V. that was a countdown to midnight. It played mellow tunes. He wondered how many other people were having their 30th at this moment? If he were watching from space, could he see their lights blinking out, one by one?

He looked outside and saw the snow was still falling. It felt like it might reach his balcony soon. If nothing else, he had certainly gotten that wish granted. He worried he may have burned all his cosmic favors on the snow. But then again, it was a beautiful backdrop to die on. The music paired with the white world outside the balcony window, it felt like they had dug out a quiet little den. They had made it. Nothing could get them here.

"May I?" Joe asked. He held out a hand to Greg. The timer had single digits on the minutes. The time had snuck up on them, but Greg was thankful for that. He placed his hand in Joe's and Joe pulled him close. They slow danced, cheek to cheek, making little circles. It didn't come as a surprise to himself, but he began to cry as they turned. Not desperate tears or sad tears, but just tears. Maybe it was fear, or maybe it was actual happiness. It had been a good day. He didn't know how long it had been since he was able to say that. Joe shushed him gently, and as the song drew to a close, he pulled away and wiped Greg's cheeks.

Joe smiled plainly and kissed Greg gently.

Greg thought of a story he had read. He was fairly certain it was an urban legend, because he had seen it a few different places with minor details changed. More often than not it took place before the internet, when everyone relied on analog clocks. The one he thought of now was a Victorian man with a waxy mustache. The article had included a photo of him as evidence that it definitely, 100%, totally happened.

It boiled down to this: a man woke up on his 30th birthday, and wound his pocket watch. He went about his day. Tied up loose ends. Had his party. He had everyone leave him before midnight, as some people still do to this day. He watched the minute hand on his watch lurch forward to midnight. He was ecstatic to see he was still alive. He threw his pocket watch to the floor. He wept and ran out the door to share the good news. A neighbor that had been at the party was on their way to bed when they saw his door fling open and no one come out. Thinking it happened by mistake, they went inside and called and called for him. But he was gone. They found his watch and realized that it was a minute fast.

The man had got to live a stolen minute. A brief window of time that might have amounted to more happiness than he had felt in his entire life. Did it matter that he ended up dying anyway? He didn't see it coming, didn't even think it a possibility. It was sad, but only to someone who was alive to know how sad it was. For the man, he went out feeling joy. It didn't seem like such a terrible way to go, Greg thought.

Maybe Greg was like that man but the reverse, he felt himself hoping. Maybe this livestream was a minute or so slow. Maybe it was already midnight and he was still alive. Still felt Joe's stubble against his lips. Would be able to call his mom to tell her the good news and feel happy in giving her that small comfort. Could call Avni and hear her squeal in excitement, Trish's colleagues be damned. Could call Peter to hear him say, "I told you I'd see you Monday. Don't forget my lucky quarter."

When the song ended, Greg realized there was just a minute left on the clock.

He felt anxiety crash on him like a wave. His neck grew hot. The tie was choking him. Seeing this, Joe grabbed the bug plush and pressed it to Greg's chest. "Our child," Joe said, trying to get Greg to laugh. Greg sniffed and tried to smile, but failed miserably. Joe drew him close and squeezed him tightly. As if he were going to keep Greg there by anchoring him to the ground.

Greg could see the countdown timer. His mind swarmed with thoughts that branched and forked like lightning racing off into the sky...

10. My own personal New Year's

9. A rocket ship set to blast off

8. Mom. Did I tell her I love her?

7. "Dying is an art, like everything else."

6. Alissa, I love you, drunk, sober, dead, or alive

5. Maybe Zeke is wherever I'll end up

4. Peter and Avni, thank you for being true friends

3. Joe, thank you for everything

2. What a waste

1. Please let me live

00:00

-30-

ABOUT THE AUTHOR

Born and raised in Bowling Green, KY, Clinton W. Waters holds a degree in Creative Writing from W.K.U. Their work has been featured in university publications from W.K.U. and the University of Regensburg. They are the lead writer for Sundog Comics and their webcomic Variants.

OTHER WORKS BY CLINTON W. WATERS

Futures Gleaming Darkly
A waiter, strapped for cash, has a watchful AI implanted before work. With a new body, an injured woman is brought face-to-face with trauma from her past. A microchip lets pet owners gain too much insight into their dog's thoughts. In his debut anthology, Futures Gleaming Darkly, Clinton W. Waters offers a window into the human experience in a world that is both mundane and fantastic. Join a host of queer characters as they navigate love, loss, and life in a technology-enhanced not-so-distant future.

Dreams Fading Brightly
Two magical bounty hunters track down their mark in the wild west. A Chosen One navigates middle-age. A border skirmish claims casualties in more ways than one. Folklore comes to life in dark forests. In a follow-up to his sci-fi collection, Clinton W. Waters provides glimpses into our world that never was. Magical realism and fantasy abound as Waters explores themes of family, duty, sacrifice, and regret, featuring a host of LGBTQ+ characters.

Unicalcarida
Autumn 1915. A revolution is taking place in the country of Walden. The mages within its borders have been declared dangerous: a drain on society in the throes of the Great War. Magic is being strangled, if not entirely stamped out. From the capital city of Waldburg in the north to Lillian's home of Bienkorb in the south, fear and paranoia reign supreme. Two young mages, Lillian and Charlotte, flee to the safety of Walden University, the stronghold of the rebel forces. They must brave the wilderness, marauding soldiers, old gods and the long shadows that are cast from within. What they learn about magic and one another along the way cannot change one simple truth - nothing will ever be the same.

Vivisection & Other Poems
Vivisection & Other Poems contains a decade of poetry from Clinton W. Waters, author of Futures Gleaming Darkly. Spanning his late teen years, throughout his time as an undergrad student at Western Kentucky University, up until the present, this collection is a roadmap of self-discovery. Waters explores his personal experiences with life, love, loss, mental illness and sexuality.

A SAMPLE FROM
FUTURES GLEAMING DARKLY

Beetle

Light glinting off of its gossamer wings, the beetle had its silver shell open, soaking in the sun. It lay dormant, but aware. The sheen of its shell was often enough to deter predators, but it attracted others. A nearby magpie garbled inquisitively. Its nest was a treasure trove of items easily taken now that there were no humans to shoo it away.

The beetle's eyes glowed faintly as it awoke. Its sunbathing would give it another day or two of use, depending on how far it traveled. The wings vibrated until they were a blur, and the beetle was on its way. It was approaching what was once a small town, its population not having as far to fall when it happened. However, the beetle had had little success in the larger cities it had visited.

Compiled in its memory were scenes of serene stillness. Cars sat silently and if it was still, it could hear every branch bending, every rat chewing fervently, plants cracking asphalt to reclaim what was theirs. At first, it reasoned that cities with more people would be more likely to have remnants, strictly speaking in terms of odds. But it had found this hypothesis was incorrect. The clustered concrete structures proved too difficult to search. It could spend an eternity thoroughly searching each room of every building. It had the time. But the beetle knew that if there were any humans left, they did not have the same luxury.

It passed through an orchard on the outskirts of the town. A scarecrow, crucified in a pumpkin patch, did not fool the beetle, but it landed on its hay-filled head. At first, these human-images had confused it. Mannequins with their frozen limbs and blank faces, dolls with their limbs at impossible angles. It wondered why the humans made such things, but decided against spending the energy on it.

The beetle investigated the nearby farmhouse. Its front door was left ajar. Inside were the signs of a hasty exit. Food was still on plates at the table, long since rotten and home to generations of flies. "Hello?" the beetle called out, just in case. A flurry of scratches filled the house as a dog scurried down the stairs and into the kitchen, its ears high, tail wagging. The dog had certainly seen better days, but it seemed to be making it without its family. It tilted its head at the beetle with its human voice.

"Sorry," the beetle said and the dog tilted its head the other way. It spread its shell once more and flew out of the house, trailed by the dog. It did not see any harm in this, so it kept its pace slow so the dog could keep up. If anything, it thought, maybe the dog could help it. The beetle could see and hear better than any human, but it could not smell.

Within a few hours, they had reached the town. Its emptiness was to be expected, but the beetle knew that its chances of success were higher at night, especially with the cooler temperatures. Any humans would need to make fire for light and heat and firelight could be seen from far away.

They inspected the town square first, finding a diner devoid of patrons. The dog was excitedly sniffing about. It located some sealed packages of food, but seemed disinterested. The beetle left it to explore the kitchen. Food sat on the flat top grill, fries were submerged in the oil of the deepfryer. If the electricity had stayed on, perhaps this building would have burnt down. A lot of them would have, the beetle conjectured.

A small room off of the kitchen appeared to be an office. The beetle tip-toed its way over piles of paper. A photograph in a silver frame showed two women and two children, posing happily in the sunshine. The beetle recognized the orchard with its pumpkin patch in the background.

The dog barked and the beetle immediately flew to it. Its tail was wagging furiously as it jumped in place. A woman stood in the doorway to the diner. The beetle landed on a nearby barstool. "Hey there," she said kindly to the dog and bent down to pet it. Her hands were bandaged.

"Hello," the beetle said, buzzing up into the air in front of her.

The woman fell back and shouted. The dog barked in concern.

"What in the hell?" she said and shielded her eyes as the beetle activated a small spotlight in its head. It saved images to its memory of her face as she squinted to see past the light. It confirmed she was one of the women from the photograph. Thinner and unkempt, but the same nonetheless.

"I am an autonomous drone that is seeking human life."

The woman got to her feet, her voice choked by tears. "Have you found anyone else? Do you know where my family is?"

"You are my first confirmed discovery to date," it told her. It turned off the spotlight and landed on the back of one of her hands. She did not wince as she drew the insect close to her face. "But it would serve my goal to find your family as well."

"And what are you supposed to do when you find us?"

"I am relaying this information currently and will have a new objective once this one is complete."

"From who? Does that mean there are others out there at least?"

"I will know more when we have completed this objective," it said. "Where might we find your family?"

"I wish I knew. I was traveling back from picking up a new refrigerator when it happened. It took me this long just to get here, but I thought it would be the best place to start looking. My wife was running the restaurant that day and the kids were at school. It's probably stupid to think she'd still be here."

The beetle processed this information. "We should continue looking. If we do not find them, we will continue to the next objective."

"Okay," she said. She took a moment to look through the building. "Let's check the school," she said. "That's the town plan for most emergencies, tornados, floods, stuff like that."

The beetle flew beside the woman, using its spotlight to light the way. The school was only a few blocks away, so they arrived shortly. They did not see any signs of life. They entered the gymnasium and it seemed that the woman had the right idea. There were sleeping bags laid out on the floor, coolers of food and water here and there between them.

The woman searched through the belongings there, but did not see anything she recognized as her wife's or her children's. They walked through the hollow halls, crayon drawings flapping lazily in a draft. The woman walked to a classroom, whose window was left open. She shut it. She lingered at a tiny desk, resting her fingers on it. "My daughter's," she said quietly. "She got sat in the front because she couldn't stop talking to her classmates."

The beetle drifted away, exploring the other classrooms. They were equally empty of people but full of their detritus, like physical echoes. Backpacks and pens and science projects. When the beetle returned, the woman and the dog were walking to the exit.

"We'll check the house next," she said to them and they followed. She found a bike leaned against the railing outside and hopped on. This considerably sped up their trip, although the woman wobbled occasionally. "It's been so long," she said to herself every time her balance betrayed her.

As they approached, the woman let out a shuddering sigh. From outside, a flickering flame could be seen inside. She jumped off of the bike and let it fall to the ground. Running up the walkway, she called out names. Attempting the door, she found that it was locked. She knocked hurriedly, desperately.

The beetle surveyed the house and found there was a gap under the backdoor that it could squeeze through. "Mom?" a voice called from another room.

"Shh!" another voice urged. The beetle could hear the woman's knocking and her voice saying their names over and over. Another woman cautiously stepped into the hallway, creeping towards the door.

"Please!" the woman outside was yelling.

The woman inside lowered herself and looked out the window. She sat down in the floor and covered her mouth, tears falling from her eyes.

The knocking at the door became a pounding sound and the woman inside covered her ears. She could not help but shriek when a bandaged fist crashed through the glass in the door. It reached in and unlocked the door from the inside as the woman skittered into the other room. The beetle followed and found the woman scooping up two small children. She ran upstairs as the door swung open.

The dog entered first, sniffing at the ground. It immediately went up the stairs, the woman following it. The beetle did not know what to make of this, so it followed, skittering across the walls.

From the doorframe, it watched as the woman placed herself between the dog and her children, brandishing a baseball bat. "Stay back!" she screamed. The dog bared its teeth at the children and the woman with the bandaged hands stood in the doorway. The children cried out in confusion.

The beetle watched as she unwound the bandages, revealing torn flesh, bones exposed. The flesh was unlike what the beetle knew of human anatomy, however. It did not bleed. The beetle received an updated objective.

It flew to the woman's neck and sank the sharp points of its feet into the skin there. The woman reached to pluck it off. The beetle discharged electricity, causing her muscles to tense and jerk. The other woman took this opportunity and brought the baseball bat against her head, tears washing her cheeks. The dog leapt forward, sinking its teeth into the weeping woman's arm.

The beetle disengaged and flew to the dog's snout. It turned on its spotlight, causing the dog to wince. The woman wrenched her arm free and the beetle delivered another surge of electricity. The dog fell to the ground, twitching.

"We should go," the beetle said and the woman, holding her bleeding arm stared at it in disbelief. She shakily reached out to touch the woman on the ground. "I recommend we leave immediately. I'm unsure if they are rendered completely dysfunctional."

The woman stood and ushered the children out of the room, promising to answer their questions as soon as possible. The beetle had used most of its energy supply, so it clung to her shoulder. She filled a backpack with food and bottled water. "Where are we going?" she asked.

"To where the objective points us. It should only be a few days, if we are quick." They set out from the house, the horizon turning orange as the sun prepared to rise. The beetle pondered as they walked. It did not know much more than the woman, but it knew that it had been tricked the same way the humans were after it happened. It would need to be more careful from now on.

If you enjoyed this preview, check out bit.ly/futuresgleamingdarkly to find out more!

Made in the USA
Middletown, DE
03 June 2022